SYRINGA

ESSENTIAL PROSE SERIES 221

Guernica Editions Inc. acknowledges the support of
the Canada Council for the Arts and the Ontario Arts Council.
The Ontario Arts Council is an agency of the Government of Ontario.

We acknowledge the financial support of the Government of Canada.

IAN ORTI

SYRINGA

GUERNICA
EDITIONS

TORONTO • CHICAGO
BUFFALO • LANCASTER (U.K.)
2024

Guernica Founder: Antonio D'Alfonso

Michael Mirolla, general editor
Julie Roorda, editor
Interior and cover design: Rafael Chimicatti
Cover image: Moises Gonzales/Unsplash

Guernica Editions Inc.
1241 Marble Rock Rd., Gananoque, ON K7G 2V4
2250 Military Road, Tonawanda, N.Y. 14150-6000 U.S.A.
www.guernicaeditions.com

Distributors:
Independent Publishers Group (IPG)
600 North Pulaski Road, Chicago IL 60624
University of Toronto Press Distribution (UTP)
5201 Dufferin Street, Toronto (ON), Canada M3H 5T8

First edition.
Printed in Canada.

Legal Deposit—Third Quarter
Library of Congress Catalog Card Number: 2023952725
Library and Archives Canada Cataloguing in Publication
Title: Syringa / Ian Orti.
Names: Orti, Ian, 1976- author.
Series: Essential prose series ; 221.
Description: Series statement: Essential prose series ; 221
Identifiers: Canadiana (print) 20230620469 | Canadiana (ebook) 20230620493
| ISBN 9781771839006 (softcover) | ISBN 9781771839013 (EPUB)
Subjects: LCGFT: Thrillers (Fiction) | LCGFT: Novels.
Classification: LCC PS8629.R84 S97 2024 | DDC C813/.6—dc23

for Ksenija

1.

Berlin / / December 31st / / 11:11pm

Shhhhhh …

Shhhhhh …

Just listen to that.

What is the name for that?

Where is the word for that?

Right there …

As her limbs break the surface of the water as she moves inside the bath.

As her arms extend to reach for the towel.

Tell me …

What is the name for the sound of the water as it falls from Syringa's skin?

Her image blurs. Vanishes with the hollow drip drip drip as the water hits the still surface. Until I open my eyes, lift my hand above the surface of the water and it's that sound again. Even if she's not here, I can still feel her skin beneath my fingertips, her flesh over the breastbone where I run my finger as though tracing the horizon across a still lake. Even now. Alone in the bath.

A continent and years away. But the more I try to hold on, the faster she vanishes, until it's a closed fist and water slipping between my fingers and again, the question:

What is the name for the sound of the water as it falls from Syringa's skin?

What word, what lexeme for the pouring of a cupped palm of water running through her hair when she once lay tangled in my legs and arms in a bathtub on a quiet winter night in Tel Aviv? What name to carry this sight the valleys of the kingdom of Heaven have nothing on? I close my eyes and try to hold on. But the last I can see of her is her back as she turns in a cream-coloured dress and the sound of the long zipper that I long ago pulled from her waist to her neck fills the room with thunder that stretches from one end of the sky to the other. Then, in the vapours of the steam above the surface of the water in the bath as moonlight cuts between the curtains, illuminating fragments of the tiles, she's gone and there's just the stillness of the water like an algae film on the surface of a pond in the hunting fields of Tiergarten, as the year closes and everything is washed out by the light, leaving nothing but my naked body here and water dripping from my hand into the tub. Then, a wind that moves in the bathroom while I slip back into narcotic slumber before being thrown awake again by the sound of her voice as she screams:

It was all a setup.

It was all a setup.

The last time I saw her, she was screaming as they pulled her out of my hotel room in Kabul. Screaming as she was dragged down a flight of stairs by her hair as my hands were bound behind my back and I could feel the heavy knee behind my neck pinning my face to the cold tiled floor. Screaming as they loaded her into a van, fists clenched behind her back, at strangers who did nothing to help her as the black sack was thrown over her head.

Water falls from the tap and echoes in this small bathroom as it falls into the tub. In hours this will all be over. So I close my eyes, struggle to find her face again. But there are only fragments. Pieces to a puzzle I will never figure out.

Outside, a thin layer of snow in the courtyard.

Berlin.

Pushing midnight.

By morning I'll be dead.

Two weeks earlier

Lungs on fire. Thighs on fire. Love on fire. I leapt two steps, three steps at a time up the stairs to the platform as I heard the train come to a stop. I'd known it was her climbing the platform for that eastbound train one stop earlier because I knew the shape of her body more than I knew my own hands. I'd memorized it, painted it and sculpted it and archived it in a library indestructible by the elements every time she stood before the wardrobe with her back to me as morning light tore through the sheer threads of the vine-embroidered curtains by the bed where I would lie and watch her dress. After a shower, when the water on her back evaporated in the morning light as she threaded her limbs through her underwear or reached high above her head for a long sweater on a wardrobe shelf for those nights when we would sit across from each other in the restaurants and let the noise cloak us like thieves, let the candlelight illuminate the lines around her eyes that I would kill a man to camp inside today. And so I knew by her face, by those eyes as green as a wild Irish mountainside, which I swear met my own before she disappeared at the top of the stairs of the platform, that it was her. I knew by the outline of her body high above me as I struggled to fit my old bicycle among the dozens of others in the snow-dusted racks outside the platform, that it was her and no one else and when our eyes met for those few moments, my body froze, and all time, in every corner of the universe, froze with me. I could hear the commuter train arriving at the platform and in the commotion of people rushing up the stairs to catch the train, I lost her. I knew the only way to catch up to her was to make it to the next stop by bike. It was a piece-of-shit bicycle which rattled and clanked but I yanked it from the rack and pointed it to the next station, riding it recklessly with fat sizzling in the quadriceps as wind burned my ears cold as I rode. I wove through pedestrians, over tram tracks, over the sidewalk and cutting off cars to reach the next station at Jannowitzbrücke as the brakes screamed to a slow stop along the tracks overhead.

I dropped the bike at the bottom of the stairs, barely able to breathe, and scrambled through people coming down, scanning each face for hers and when I made it to the platform at the top of the stairs I wedged my arm between the sliding doors and screamed as the pain shot through my elbow, shoulder, and neck as the door closed on the abscess on my forearm. I was able to wiggle into the car as it departed. I hadn't moved like that in ages and it felt like someone had taken a flamethrower to my lungs. But finally, finally, after all this time, after all these miles travelled, oceans crossed, or cities ransacked, over the benches I'd made my bed when walking became impossible, after the airports, train stations, and run-down hotel rooms, I finally came face to face with her, on the other side of the glass, walking alone down the platform, the last off the lead car, and I, the last on the end car as it slowly pulled away from the station. I slammed my hand against the window to get her attention and I swear that for a second, she saw me too.

"But it wasn't her," Hissel said, with his scratchy voice.

"It's never her," I said. "I see her everywhere and she is nowhere. I look everywhere and find nothing. The back of her neck as she descends the stairs to the subway, the blue vein threaded over the tendons in her wrists that poke beneath her jacket as she leans down to lift a suitcase before boarding a train. But I am always too late and she is never there. It was crazy to think it was her — my vision is bad and getting worse. This whole city is a blur now and I can barely tell one face from another anymore. But still, I know I saw something."

I stayed on the train and when it reached the last stop, I stayed where I was as others got off and when the lights went out in the train I found myself trembling, my tears propelled by the exhaustion of years searching for her. I closed my eyes and cursed that red S-Bahn commuter train, one more in the brutal sum of one-way tickets on busses, trains, and planes, of nights standing alone at gates and on platforms hoping the next ride would finally be the one that led to her. I added that empty, run-down wagon, where my lungs now ached from the race to get to her, to the mountain of suitcases packed hastily in the night, to the rides in the back of taxis, to the countless times staring out the window with an empty seat beside me without her head resting on my lap. I'd lost track of how many nights I'd spent in trains speeding past in the night, how many horizons where the sky was just breaking that I imagined this would be the day that broke on me finding her only to search and find nothing. I'd searched everywhere for her. Turned over every rock, kicked in every door, shook down everyone I thought might have answers. I lost count of the number of times wanting to give up but not being out of love enough to do it.

I wiped my face as the lights came back on the train. In my shit vision I could squint and at least make out a single-digit number on the board so I knew the train would leave again soon enough and head westward back to the city. I stayed in my seat with my eyes closed until I felt the train start again. A few stops in, a young couple in their teens or early twenties boarded and sat across from me. I stared across the aisle at their wiry young frames as the train jolted us from side to side as it slowly entered the city, past the large and monotonous *plattenbaus,* past the clusters of *schrebergartens,* the cottage communes scattered

throughout Berlin dotted with satellite dishes and the flags of
local football clubs. Eventually the Spree River came into view.
I was strangely at home in Berlin. It was alive and dead at the
same time. Berlin was a city of ghosts, where there was nothing
that couldn't keep on living somehow. Amusement parks and
airports died and were reborn here and military no-man's lands a
generation ago were now wide-open fields alive and ornamented
with bodies entwined on picnic blankets amidst the low hum
of a far off portable stereo speaker and the popping of caps off
cheap night-market beer bottles. The young couple across from
me were oblivious to me. They were listening to music, sharing
a set of ear-buds they each had in one ear. I knew that soon they
would devour each other because I'd once sat in that very seat before. With gangly legs, and gangly arms, with a smooth face and a
jacket pocket full of cassettes, rolling papers and a dry ball of hash
in a matchbox, enough change for a bus or a corner-store beer
and yet still feeling the wealth of an emperor. I admired them,
safely close enough to the end of my own life to feel anything re-
sembling envy. They didn't need money or property when they
had the vast landscape of each other's bodies. They were like two
low-flying comets with the city passing so quickly in the window behind them, enveloped in that sacred orb of youth, which
for a short time is impenetrable by the past or future, until both
make an endless meal of it. But for now, it was a beautiful sight.
Somewhere along the ride the two young lovers vanished, crashing to the earth in the bed of some basement apartment beneath
blankets that would go unwashed till spring when they emerged
and their skinny legs would walk them, with a bedsheet or picnic
blanket in tow, to the windy fields along the abandoned airport
runways in Templehofer Field where the grass goes uncut for
ages and the sun takes forever to set. I was exhausted and starv-
ing when I finally arrived back at my flat but I was too tired to eat.
I was thirsty but too tired to reach for a glass. I held my lips to the
kitchen faucet and sucked in cold water. My ankles, knees, and

hips ached so I walked to the bathroom, peeled off my clothes, ran the water in the bath and climbed in immediately.

I reached my arm forward to turn off the water when the bath was finally full and through the fog of the water or my exhaustion, I saw Hissel there, with those eyes again, sitting across from me, as though we were back on the train. I saw the Reichstag through the window behind him, its geodesic dome faintly lit beneath the low hanging clouds. I saw that long beard of his. The jean jacket he never unbuttoned once. The sweatpants and builder's boots. I felt them in the tub against my naked feet and saw the tears running down his cheeks.

I squeezed my fist and saw that the burst blood vessels once purple and blue on my arm were now a darker red along the edges. Beneath the surface of the skin I could feel the bulbous vein, the tight infectious pocket of blood slowly spreading beneath the skin from where I'd dared the needle to pass beneath my skin the night before and strike the vein. It was a thing I did to stay on top of the habit. I'd load the needle with gear, then hold it like a pen between my thumb and forefinger and, starting at the wrist, I would climb my forearm, slowly and shallowly puncturing the epidermis. I'd make my way up my forearm like the devout climbing the ninety-nine steps of St. Joseph's Oratory in Montreal, taking each step on their knees in the hopes of a miracle from the ghost of the resident friar. I never went up those ninety-nine steps on my knees when I lived in Montreal but I had taken in my share of chilly sunsets from the observation terrace at the entrance to the Basilica where a kind of solace was possible, steps from the cavernous rooms where inside sat the vacated wheelchairs and crutches of those who'd sought miracles and claimed to have received. From my wrist, I'd count out ninety-nine steps, holding the needle between the epidermis and subcutaneous tissue, occasionally drawing blood. Last night I'd held the needle there at the top of my forearm, the way I'd held the view of St. Joseph's, with the sun right there but out of reach, before finally giving in and burying my thumb into the plunger and feeling thirty-five trillion cells dissolve into the night.

3.

Berlin. New Year's Eve. 11: 59pm

There are defence mechanisms to prolong the life of a drowning man or woman. Mammalian diving reflexes. Means to slip the body into energy reserve mode to maximize the time spent under water. Bradycardia. Drastic reduction in the heart rate. Peripheral vasoconstriction, or the restriction of blood flow to the extremities so vital organs stay supplied with oxygen. Finally, a blood shift to the thoracic cavity to maintain integrity of the lungs and diaphragm to prevent collapse as the pressure increases as the body sinks.

Next comes the thrashing. The body's wild disguise as a fight for life when it's really death's accelerant, a means to exhaust the heart and reduce suffering.

When I was a child, I fell through the ice in Lake Ontario. When lakes froze thick enough to drive the cars across them. We'd done just that, my father's car the last in a convoy crossing the two-kilometre channel for a birthday party on Wolfe Island. I remember my mother telling him to take the ferry but my father insisted on following his cousins across the frozen lake. "They do it all the time," he'd said. But the earth was changing beneath our noses, and no one noticed until it was too late. I remember the wide snow-covered lake and the tire tracks blown over with drifting snow in front of us. The determined look in my father's eyes and his occasional glance through the rear-view mirror. Then the way my mother pressed her fingers to the window when we heard the crack and felt the sudden drop. As though, with those pale slender fingers, she could push back a lake. For a while I believed that she could. The last thing I remember is the sight of her fingers on that window from where I was sitting in the back seat, though the newspaper says I was pulled by divers from her lap within an hour of the car going through the ice. Despite her mammalian reflexes, my mother did not survive. Nor did my father, whose body was missing from the car but found in spring downstream from where we'd broken through the ice. He'd made it out from the car but was pinned beneath the ice.

I close my eyes, lower my ears beneath the water in the bathtub where my breath feels as loud as waves crashing on the coast. Through the water I hear footsteps in the courtyard through the open windows and that click click click of a woman's shoes on the sidewalk becomes the tick tick tick of a bedside watch as the stray dogs chase away cats and the chickens in the cantina below in a time long before now.

Where am I now? Where is this thick air, this tropical humidity that makes the sheets stick to my skin as I roll on to my side? The thin white drapes twirl in the breeze as the small engines of motorbikes, the motor of the unrepaired fridge, all hum and clang amid and the low drones of the fishing boats outside. It could be any day. I hear the taps squeak shut and the door is open a crack in the bathroom. Enough to see your dark limbs and narrow waist, the long soft ridges of your ribcage as water that trails from your hair down the entirety of your body glistens as it catches the sun.

Why leave the door open? Because you want me to see you? For all you know I'm asleep. But the answer is simple. The door is open on our youth. What are we now? Nineteen? Wearing our nudity with the innocence of children but our sexuality like stars on the shoulders of generals. We are refugees but we don't know it yet. Safe from the future we've not yet been enlisted to die for. Free now, in the past, from a future we've not even begun to consider. We eat for fuel that's spent beneath the bedsheets, torching molecules of carbon our bodies have chopped down from the food at roadside stands just to sustain an existence that for a burning short time feels utterly unstoppable. Our needs are shelter and privacy. A bed and a side-table are enough for furniture. The clothes are scattered and need to be washed. We're long before the slow march in furniture shops. We'll wash our clothes in the sink, sweat through the sheets, shower together, and spend the afternoon playing cards on the bed in our damp towels. We'll get on a plane and never look back once, get on a bus until the last stop, drink on trains and draw the curtains and sink into the darkness and each other's bodies and then hop off when we smell the ocean. We'll inhabit the present tense alone and never turn back to see how quickly the past just turns to mist. The fleet of beds an archipelago, our world beyond the everyone and everything, but as delicate as the threads of these sheets on the brink of tearing open a hole to an inhospitable future which we can both see awaits us. In time, this will all be over and we'll not be together. We both sense it but we say nothing. But it's there nonetheless, uncoiling in the silence whenever we dress, and so we almost never dress.

But these strange rooms will always be here. When time fissures and the past opens up again the way the earth cracks open and swallows men when the pressure beneath the surface becomes too great for even the mountains to bear. The window of the car flying down the highway where in the back seat you took my hand and slid it between your legs beneath your steel blue dress, is somehow always open. The window into our bedroom as we disappear beneath the sheets, is somehow always open, there for us to peer inside or crawl through when the hair is turning grey and the lines are getting deeper in the face and the body slows and the healing takes longer and the hangovers are so bad you just avoid the drink altogether, and the bedtime is earlier because staying up all night is arduous and avoided at all costs because there's nothing left in darkness of the night that hasn't already been discovered, and the meals are square and lungs are free from the tobacco and hash and we're packing the kids' lunch and we're stuck in traffic on the way to work and the bills are late and the eyes are heavier and heavier and you've been gone for so long. And you've been gone for so long.

These spaces still live on in the cartography of love. These windows and doors always there to be open. Into a room where you're stepping out of a shower into a world that's long left us now and your hair is long and wet and there's no tomorrow or yesterday, just an ever-growing room bill and a warm Pacific wind twirling the drapes like the ghosts of a dervish as you open the door and you're just a silhouette behind the morning light and you open your mouth to speak but instead of words comes blinding light, a terrifying explosion and when I open my eyes again there's just the dim light from the candles and the flickering tiles in the bathroom and the hissing of a few spent fireworks casings set off by some kids in the courtyard.

It will be months before they find my body and it will not be a pretty sight. With the birdshit all around me. With mosquito eggs in my rotted nostrils. Any number of insects will have settled in my hair and ears to spawn their young. And in my decaying gaping mouth I'll hear the crack of pigeon egg as a hatchling sees light for the first time.

4.

Berlin. November 11

I sat outside with Hissel. The place was a cross between café and bar. We were the only ones sitting outside and there were folded red blankets draped on the backs of the empty chairs. He sat with the blanket from his chair wrapped around his shoulders as I told him the story of the fire in Kabul and the last night I saw Syringa. I was spare with the details. She'd been working as a schoolteacher at a girls school. I didn't know if this was real or a cover and I didn't ask. There'd been a fire at the school so gruesome it took international headlines and she'd come to me with accusations that went beyond the official story of an accident.

"Is this why you think she was taken away?" he asked.

"There were two versions of the fire. The one people read about and her version."

"Killed by a fire that never touched her."

"It touched her. When we ran into each other over there she told me there were things she needed to tell me and asked if we could meet in private. I thought it would be about something else. About us. About her. But she was different. She'd shed the skin I once knew her in. Layers and layers and layers of it."

Hissel didn't move under that blanket as I spoke. He sat dead still as I fidgeted with my cigarettes.

"She trusted you," he said.

"It wasn't the first time she'd come to me with a story she implored me to write. Years earlier a Canadian major was killed when a bomb had fallen on top of his bunker clearly marked U.N. The story went page one but not her version of it. The story had some traction for a while but everyone was barking up the wrong tree. Her version — that it had been done with the knowledge and blessing of the major's Prime Minister — could never see the light of day."

"Why not?"

"It just wouldn't. They classified what was left of the file to make sure it never would."

"But you knew the truth."

"Did I? It was a conspiracy she'd brought me, on a scratchy phone call in the middle of the night of all things. It was a great way to torpedo my career. She didn't get that. I didn't even know where she was calling from. When I woke up in the morning it was like it had never happened. My only source was 'caller unknown.'"

"Maybe second time was different."

"I was hoping she'd reached out for another reason. That maybe part of her just wanted to see me again, story or no story. To start over maybe, but there was nothing to start over. She insisted this fire was bigger than the two of us and it annoyed me to hear her say this. She was frantic about it all. She said she was taking a chance coming to me, but I snapped and told her she sounded like a fanatic flying off the deep end."

Hissel was quiet for a moment. "You pissed her off."

"I missed her. I didn't want to talk about news or sources or the truth, whatever that meant."

"She was probably desperate. Maybe she saw you as refuge. Or the story as her way out. You write story. Things settle. Maybe go back to normal."

"I wasn't seeing clearly. If we'd had more time maybe I would have. You can't think clearly there. The place comes at you from every angle. She said so herself that she was at the end of her rope. She'd stomached the fact that what she knew about Lebanon and the bunker would never be public, but this was different, especially considering who these victims were. She was too close. She'd attended their birthday parties. Held them in her arms. A maverick major in with fateful emails to his wife about war crimes was one thing. Dead schoolgirls was another."

"And so, you betray her by not running the story she died to bring you."

"The story meant nothing to me with her gone. And she wasn't just gone, she was erased. Vanished. They took her that night. Before my eyes. And nothing I could have written would have set her free or brought her back."

"You could still write story. Tell everything. Tell the truth."

"I couldn't have cared less about the truth after that," I said. "Besides, stories have sources. The source of this story was worse than dead — she no longer existed. The spin was already on. The official version was the version everyone wanted to hear — an act of terror and an injection of resources to right it — and the public ate it up."

Hissel listened as I continued.

"So no, there was no story. But that doesn't mean there is no ending. I have names. God knows if they're the right ones but they're the last things she ever gave me."

"Tell me about this dead lover's list."

"Two or three names. One name she tapped at with her finger when I wrote it. If he was behind the fire, then it made sense that if he knew she'd come to me, that he was behind her disappearance too. I traced him here where he'd recently been stationed. But the name is all I have. No one I could pick out of a crowd with the pictures that exist of him."

"Who else?" Hissel asked.

I gave him the name and he said, "Why him?" and I told him. That this man worked at the embassy and had refused to help me when I reached out to him the night we were both arrested. That this man let me sit in a prison for three days and then signed off on my deportation when I was able to prove to him that she was alive and real. He was the reason I was now in Berlin. He was private sector now, a consultant for a think tank, but hosting a party for some diplomats on New Year's Eve.

"Where?"

"I don't know yet."

"Ha!" Hissel said, chortling. "No invitation for you."

"I'll find it."

"You're lost."

He annoyed me because he was right. I was lost. Of all the cities
in the world, I'd managed to find the right one, but still I was a
fool. I took a cigarette from the package on the table and offered
him one but he declined with a slight wave of his gloved hand.
I lit mine, and exhaled slowly. "It was odd that I would run into
her again," I said. "And there, of all places. That we would meet
again, anywhere, stars had to align. That we would meet in the
same city in Afghanistan of all places was different. I saw her in
a market and neither of us could turn away. I walked toward her,
but she stepped away from me not letting me show any sign of
affection there. Instead, she stepped beside me in that crowded
market and pressed her shoulder against mine. I knew she was
happy to see me. It was strange but I just stood there and let her
lean against me and said nothing. But then she pulled me into a
less crowded stall filled with stacks of folded clothing wrapped
in plastic and suddenly there was something like shock or dis-
trust that came over her. She asked me what I was doing there
but cut me off with more questions before I could answer. Like
I said, she was different. Our conversation became rushed or
forced or awkward there in the market. She left the stall and I
followed her to a more crowded section of the market. I tried to
be discreet and got close to her but when I said a few words to
her in English, she turned away like she couldn't understand me.
For a moment I lost her in the crowd and I couldn't figure out
what was going on, but moments later, I felt her body against
mine. We were shoulder to shoulder as she leaned over to look at
an object on sale at the stall. She said we should meet right away
and she said it was urgent — that she needed to tell me things. I
couldn't get a read on her, but I wrote down my phone number
on a small piece of paper and left it on the edge of a table in the
stall. Looking back, I think because I was there, and that it was
so impossible that I should be there with her, that she believed

that our meeting had to have been orchestrated somehow, as a test for her."

"A test how?"

"She knew things she couldn't keep secret anymore and she needed to tell someone, and she knew she could tell me. Or maybe I was just her last gamble on someone she could trust. I didn't know what to make of anything. The exhaustion, the place, the heat, the cold, everything was making her paranoid. Nothing is stable there. Paranoia is a survival mechanism in some lines of work, but it can't be sustained without slowly killing you. It strips you down. Unravels you. If I had been sent there to test her loyalty or as bait, then it was without my knowing. I never had any instructions but to nose out a story for a magazine back home and take a few photos. Maybe looking back that was an ambiguous assignment but I was able to do it. I'd been all over the world on all kinds of assignments, writing stories as they came. But for the two of us to meet there. In that market. Maybe I should have seen it. You meet in hometown cafés after ten years or in a mall buying clothes for your teenage kid. Not fourteen months after the way we'd parted halfway around the globe."

There was a long pause as Hissel stared straight ahead.

"Maybe she just saw you and saw a way out."

I pulled on the cigarette as we both stared straight ahead as I told him what happened our final night together. "The night they dragged her away it was local police. To them she was as a married woman, a teacher with a husband away working. She couldn't travel with men so being seen with me alone in a hotel was grounds enough for them. I thought the embassy could help her. But I sat in that cell for days without access to anyone. When

I finally saw someone from the embassy, he only wanted to know what she'd been so anxious to tell me. When I got out, I read about the fire, but the official version was far from hers and their denying her existence was all the validation I needed. Everyone knew she was in the country. I had text messages, I even had photos which I'd taken of her in the market. Everything confirmed it and everyone denied they knew her. Including the man who'd come to see me when I'd cornered him in the embassy shortly after I was finally let out and told to board the next plane out. No one would help. I did everything I could to find her. But I was deported. I fought tooth and nail to stay. I called fixers, diplomats, any contact I had. I was cut off. No one would talk to me. And when they did, they said there was no record of her. But I had pictures of her. There. On those streets. But it meant nothing. She was gone and I had nothing."

Hissel kept the blanket around his shoulders the whole time while I lit cigarette after cigarette.

"It's good what you did. You tried. It would mean something to her to know that," Hissel said, breaking the long silence. "It would mean everything."

"In the end it means nothing."

Hissel smiled a bit, trying to lighten up the mood. "Maybe you should have written story. Maybe you win big award. Maybe life is better for you."

"And then what?"

"Who knows? Book deal? A position somewhere teaching journalism? Stability," Hissel said. "Some calm for you here." He tapped his head.

"I'm fine up here," I said, tapping my head. But we both knew I wasn't. "Let's say you're right, and she came to me for help because she saw me as a way out. Then what? What was the way out I gave her? What was the door I opened? A trap-door to Hell."

"You shouldn't be so hard on yourself."

I butted the cigarette out in the ashtray and pulled a passport from my breast pocket.

"Tell me something. Look long at this photo. Do you recognize this person?"

Hissel held the passport in his hand and was silent. He stared at the photo, passing his thumb over the photo over and over.

"Handsome guy."

I held the passport photo to my face and let him see the two faces, how the one in front of him speaking looked a hundred years older than the one in the photograph. "Maybe you're right. Maybe I'm not fine up here. But I know what I want. Enough fucking around, Hissel. You can do this for me or you can't. If not, fuck off, and I'll find someone else."

He lifted his glasses and rubbed his eyes with his fingers, wiped his nose with a napkin on the table and coughed a dry cough. He clicked his loose dentures together a few times.

"You must think you're lucky," he said. "The first crazy vet you find on the street is going to help you kill somebody."

"You must think *you're* the lucky one. You'll never see money like this in your life again."

His voice was dry.

"You're a major novice. But I like you." He let out a laugh that turned into a bronchial cough. "This weather. I'm getting sick. I should go."

"I'm serious," I said.

I put my passport in my breast pocket and lit another cigarette.

"There is sauna you should go to," he said.

"I feel fine."

"No. You're not fine. It will clear your head. And it will be good for whatever circulation you have left." He wrote the name of the sauna on the paper I'd given him and handed it back to me. Then he handed me a napkin with the pen.

"Write the name of man you think you need."

I took the pen and wrote on the napkin.

"This two names."

"The first is the name she gave me. The spook behind the fire. The other is the diplomat who came to see me when I was being detained over there. He's here now too."

"You think there's a connection?"

"I don't care if there's a connection."

Hissel folded the napkin and put it in his pocket. "We all die. Why you need me? Go home. Save your money."

I rose from my seat and he grabbed my arm but I pulled it away, trying to hide the pain from where he had grabbed me. He could see I was agitated.

"Wait," he said. "One last question."

"What?"

"If you could go back in time to that night, night she come to you over there, night she was taken away, what would you do?"

"What does this have to do with anything?"

"Amuse me. A good answer, good results for you."

I shook my head and turned away from Hissel. The pavement was wet, and I could feel the temperature had dropped a few degrees. "I would touch her," I said. "It's stupid I know. We never touched, other than those few moments she leaned into me at the market. We'd met in the market, then she came in the door with her story, pacing around the room. And then she was gone. She could have been a ghost for all I know had I not felt the weight of her body against mine for those few seconds in the market. I would touch her. Her face, her hands. Anything."

"Go to the sauna tomorrow night. I will check names. See if your girl is ghost or not. Close your eyes. Breathe. Sweat. Get that poison out of your body." Hissel pointed to my sleeve. "And go to doctor. Your arm is infected. Soon, with necrosis they will cut it off. Maybe I can help you. But I need your head clear if I do. I'll be there. Maybe we talk more."

"My head is clear," I said.

"Your head is clear. You think your government make news magazine hire you to take pictures in faraway land to test loyalty of spy
woman."

"Maybe."

"Yes, maybe," Hissel said, nodding. "And maybe just stars align."

He stayed in the seat as I dropped money on the small table between us. Neither of us said goodbye as I left. The rest of the day
I walked until I found the bar near the Volkspark where I knew
I could score. It didn't take long and afterwards I entered an old
GDR-era cinema nearby and bought a ticket for the first film on
the board. It was early evening and only a few people were in
the lobby. I bought two bottles of beer and a small popcorn and
walked up the wide carpeted staircase to the theatre. I was completely alone in the theatre and took a seat in the middle. Soon
the lights went out and the film began but I paid no attention
to it. The image flickered and the people on-screen spoke but I
heard nothing. I didn't touch the popcorn — I barely ate anything anymore and it showed. I held the beer in my hand and
closed my eyes. When I opened them, she was there on screen.
Metres high. Taking up the entire width of my view. In every fe-
male character on the screen I could see her. In the lead, her. In
the lead's child, her. In the extras walking in the streets in the
background, her, her, her. And when they buried the old woman
at the end of the film, her. But I also saw Hissel up there on
screen, always in the background, looking straight at me. I closed
my eyes and when I opened them again a theatre employee was
standing over me lightly shaking me. I walked back to my flat,
shielding my face from the rain until a tram came into view, and
even on the tram I couldn't stop shivering. When I got back to

my flat, I peeled off my wet clothes and ran the bath. When I left
Hissel at the café earlier that day, with the red blanket draped
around his shoulders, after he'd pressed me about the final day
with Syringa and stared straight ahead still under that blanket,
I turned around before rounding a corner and watched him.
His hands had emerged from beneath that red blanket and he
reached into the ashtray where'd I'd left a half-dozen cigarette
butts. I stood there and watched him, sure he couldn't see me.
He lifted the cigarette butt to his lips but never lit it. He just held
it there in his lips, which tightened around the filter like he was
softly inhaling. He did it repeatedly with his eyes closed and his
little arm disappeared back under the blanket. I tried to forget
everything in the bathtub. I thought about loading the syringe
and burying the needle straight into the centre of my heart.
Instead, I rolled some hash with some old tobacco on a tin beside the bath. I was good with gear in general, but I was feeling
destructive after meeting with Hissel and stuck with the hash as
a way to tell myself I had everything under control. I'd achieved
a kind of perfect symbiosis to drugs any outsider would call de-
nial or a problem. As a journalist who got assignments to coun-
tries where the rope went tight around the necks of users, there
was a self-discipline required that came with the job and it took
little more than few days in a locked hotel room with a steady
supply of cigarettes, alcohol, and ibuprofens to set things right
when the body got hungry for what it wasn't allowed to have.
My bones would ache with what felt like a flu sent by the most
vindictive gods, but it would always be over in a few days. Painful
as it was, there was no denying that the gear, when right, when
proper, when pure and uncut, foregrounded the cosmic unity of
everything around me and of which I was both the centre and
spectator. How the rubber tires of a car unhindered on a long
street at night was also the gentle ebb of the sea at low tide. How
the grinding curve of a late-night tram spoke for a far-off thunder. It was all nature. It was all the reverse refraction of colour

into a prism and everything coming out in a single unified beam of light. A car bomb or a bursting geyser, a demolition site or a landslide. There was nothing in the machine world that wasn't also nature. There was no human emotion that didn't have a twin somewhere in the wilderness. I'd been volcanic and I'd been the stillness of the sky reflected in the ice of a frozen lake blown clear of snow. I was the salmon swimming upstream, climbing waterfalls with cool water rushing against the silver scales of my back, gliding unscathed between the wooden claws of a Kodiak, past icy rocks smoothed centennially by the waters of my birth, where through the still shallow waters I bathed in the light of Aurora Borealis. But even when the gear was good, nature's contract, that everything, everywhere had its end, would have to be honoured, and, like the salmon, I would decompose, feel the otter's teeth gnashing at my insides while I endured the slow suffocation of life on dry land.

But Hissel was right and my arm was becoming a problem; if I didn't treat it, I would lose it. The next day, I visited a clinic, and the abscess on my arm was mercilessly drained and then bandaged. I was given an aggressive round of antibiotics and a blunt lecture on self-abuse. But I wasn't there to save my arm. I just needed to buy time and couldn't risk slipping into some feverish infection to knock me off course.

In the following days, alone in my flat, I fought to control the images, to lock Syringa away. But I'd close my eyes and she'd be there, dressing by the window, lifting a bra strap over her shoulder, or pulling back her hair, then I'd lose her in the dust kicked up by the jeeps in Kabul, in the sun that set behind the cross on the mountain in Montreal, in the stones in the river in Kyoto, and the seawater on our faces standing waist deep in the ocean as the sun rose over the waves cresting over the horizon. She'd be gone. And then I'd feel her again, her breath on my lips, before she was gone again, and the other images, sounds, and sensations came flooding in. Hissel's face as he held those old cigarettes to his lips, and then the screaming of children, and the feeling that my skin was on fire.

5.

Berlin. September 21

The very first time I met Hissel was the last day of summer. I was on a bridge overlooking a canal in Kreuzberg. The trees had only just begun to turn colour and it was still quite warm. I was standing there when I felt someone's hand on my shoulder. He startled me as I stood watching the boats pass beneath the bridge. When I turned around, he was staring at me and the butt of his hand was resting on my throat. His hand was trembling against my throat. The sun was in my eyes and I couldn't make out his face clearly. There were deep lines in his face and he stared at me as though in disbelief. He just stood there, with that shaking hand and trembling lips beneath that thin long beard, in a jean jacket and construction boots, and eyes behind lightly tinted sunglasses.

"My instinct was to kill you," he'd said in a weathered, raspy voice, as he patted my shoulder to let me know he was no longer a threat. I said thanks and stood there, trying to size him up in case he changed his mind. His face was so worn it almost appeared prosthetic in the light. He kept his eyes on me, then moved them downwards and apologized but kept his hand on my shoulder.

"You don't remember me, do you?" There was a reserved desperation in his voice.

"No."

"Why should you?" he'd said. "You just look like a man I know."

"I get that a lot. I have one of those faces."

I felt his fingers tighten on my shoulder and I held still. I'd seen his kind. Reported on them. Photographed them. Afghan war throwaways. Ex-NATO, ex-contractor, ex-NGO, and ex-journalists, ravaged by an over-abundance of drugs and a faith long dead in a mission over a decade old. Men tired of places where the law changed in each village if it even existed at all. He could have been full of shit, but he fit the description and asked for nothing. No money. Nothing. To calm him down and ease his grip on my shoulder I suggested we walk and so we walked. He stumbled a bit and we rested on a bench and I let him tell his story, never questioning him about whether he'd actually been where he said he had been. He said he'd done two tours. Afghanistan. He had the small details. Stuff inside the barracks and the compounds that never went reported in magazines. He joked about trading ration kits, and how the Bulgarian soldiers had the worst ones and the Danes the best. He even went through their menu, then trailed off about the sticks of cinnamon gum given to the Afghan cleaning staff inside the bases and how they thought their mouths were on fire and that the soldiers would get a kick out of it. He just seemed like a man who wanted to talk. I had no friends, and I'd barely spoken more than the words to order coffee or lunch in weeks. We spoke and his story became more believable the more he went on. He named places that I knew and even a few journalists who were working there. He said he was, or had been, a soldier, though he was far from looking the part now. He was very thin, but his grip on my shoulder at the bridge had been strong and the way he'd held my chin up with the butt of his fist on my throat was convincing enough. I tested him and suggested we'd met across the border in Uzbekistan near where German troops were stationed but he said no one was allowed off the base alone, let alone across the border. He gave details about the business he knew was straddling the border and they matched mine. His memory was probably better than mine at the time as I was almost as much a part of the story

I was covering, watching the black jeeps cross the Friendship Bridge loaded with heroin en route to Europe. What came over raw was processed in Uzbekistan and I'd let myself get sucked into what fell conveniently off the back of those trucks. After being deported, Uzbekistan was the closest I could get to Afghanistan though I knew it made no sense to go back there and I knew deep down there was nothing I would turn up. When the army says you don't exist, and your country denies any record of you, and when the last thing anyone ever saw of you was a black sack going over your head after being dragged down a flight of stairs by your hair, your status is ex-human.

When I finally made it back to the region it was through Uzbekistan, where I'd entered as one man and left as another. I arrived determined to get back across the border to find a woman I knew deep down was dead. To distract myself from a reality that I felt in the marrow of my bones, I worked. I sustained myself writing for magazines that prospered on the kind of drugsploitation stories in exotic destinations I was sending them back, entirely falsified. I took photos of street vendors or grocers who worked metres from my hotel, men with gaunt and weathered faces who I cast as pimps and dealers across central Asia for stories that would be touted as edgy journalism but there was nothing I would write from there that would ever be fact-checked if it could be click-baited into revenue instead. The only thing that was true was the product I was writing about. But still, I was focused enough to know there were two names I'd been left with and that never left me. They couldn't. I'd etched each one into my mind and trawled whatever media I could get my hands on, crossing names off the list that didn't add up. But there were always two. The man whose name she'd feverishly tapped on the paper the night she was taken away and the man who visited me in prison concerned with only what she'd told me. I had no idea what he did or what she knew but there was a straight line that ran from him to the school fire and it ran right through her. I discovered he'd taken a position in Berlin and soon after, like a goddamn Christmas gift, caught his name in the caption of an event photo, a public relations soccer game with members of the embassy and a refugee sports club in Berlin, a security detail in a diplomatic entourage. I'd moved back to Montreal, a wreck, and slowly shut my life down, selling everything I could to sustain the life I was planning to set up in Berlin. I got totally clean which meant no more than a six-pack a day and a fistful of hash for the month. I took losses on everything I sold but I didn't care. The goal was Berlin, for an event on New Year's Eve. I was moving too fast for it to matter that I had no means and no experience pulling off a job like this. I had money. And I had the wherewithal that comes with knowing this was the last thing I'd ever do. I'd been around enough of the right people, soldiers, fixers, and even insurgents to know which buttons to press. It's how I tested Hissel when I met him. It would have been easy to let myself get seduced by the convenience of our meeting. But I was convinced he really had been a soldier. That he was off the grid gave me leverage. He was unstable and never gave up more than his first name and wagged his finger whenever I asked for details about his battalion. The fact he was so skinny suggested he'd been behind a desk. That he wasn't suggested he'd been worn down the same way I had. When I brought it up later how I found it serendipitous that we'd met, he said again, "Maybe just stars align." We were a perfect match: a soldier on the run from a trio of political bodies, and a suicidal fuckup commissioning a trio of assassinations including his own, though I kept Hissel in the dark about the last part.

Hissel's story, according to Hissel that afternoon, was that he'd once refused an order that changed the course of his life, but it was impossible to know if he was telling the truth. It seemed far more likely he'd been discharged. It was hard for him to get the same version of the story out when I pressed him for details. Whatever it was, he was cagey about it. "I just met you," he'd tell me. But this was a lie. Our meeting on the bridge was no coincidence. He'd been following me for weeks.

6.

Berlin. November 12

I followed the long gravel driveway into the alley where a woman dressed in loose white pants and T-shirt was carrying a bin of white towels into a laundry room. The sauna was quiet. I undressed in the open change room and fastened the wristband with the key and locker number to my wrist. Nearby a woman was undressing and when she saw the dark cellulitis beneath the bandage on my forearm, she looked away and I draped the towel over my arm and walked to the shower area. The place was dark, and smelled of citrus and herbs and inside the sauna area I could see a man pouring water over the rocks and filling the small wooden room with steam. I showered under hot water at the other side of the room. Close to the open showers was a small cement pool filled with ice cold water, enough to hold one person only. I climbed in and lowered myself into the water, holding on to the edge and took slow quiet breaths. I looked around the open room for Hissel but I couldn't see him. A few naked bodies exited the sauna area and the scent of citrus grew. One or two more people exited but none were Hissel. I rose from the cold waters of the small cement pool and walked slowly to the closed wooden enclosure and opened the glass door. I sat naked on the long white towel among five or six other naked men and women and fiddled with the wristband with my locker number and key on it and then closed my eyes and let the sweat pour slowly down my face. When I opened them I tried to make out Hissel but I still could not. The steam was thick and the room was barely lit but I would not have missed that beard. The intense heat felt good and I lowered my head and closed my eyes again until I heard the door open and saw a woman enter. I felt the bench sink slightly

under the weight of her long dark legs as she stepped beside me
and sat directly behind me where the heat was most intense. I
stayed in as long as I could, occasionally lifting my head to see
if I could see Hissel but he was not there and there was barely
enough light coming in the room from the window behind me
where the woman sat. It was no matter. His suggestion to come
here was only that — a suggestion, and so there was no reason to
expect him. In the dark the damaged blood vessels on my forearm
were not visible and I was able to relax. I sat until someone returned with a bucket and some different herbs and soon the heat
became overwhelming as he performed some small ceremony,
pouring water from a wooden ladle over the rocks and spinning
a towel over his head to circulate the intense heat. I opened the
heavy glass door when he concluded, barely able to breathe, and
left the small room with its wooden slat benches and walls and
took another door nearby to a quiet outside courtyard adjacent
the sauna and let the cold air pass over my body. I stood under a
small shower head attached to a flimsy pipe coming out of the
ground and turned the tap to let cold water fall over my chest and
shoulders for a few moments. When I turned around, I could
faintly see the outline of the woman who had been sitting behind
me looking back at me through the thin window. I couldn't see
her face through her long wet hair hanging past her shoulders so
maybe she wasn't looking at me at all but was just looking outside — as though the sight of the snowy courtyard could cool
her down inside all of that thick steam. I sat down in an extended
chair with a towel around my waist as the snow fell softly in the
courtyard. Steam rose from my limbs in the cold air. The courtyard was narrow and protected by a high red brick wall on one
side and a tall wooden fence with climbing ivy on the other side.
In the middle of the courtyard, next to the shower pipe climbing
out of the ground stood a thin young sapling which provided a
small canopy over the shower. Surrounding the tree was a square
path made of small white stones. I lay in the chair watching snow

fall around me. When I finally cooled off, I went back into the sauna. There was still no sight of Hissel and the woman who had been sitting behind me in the darkness was gone too. I moved in and out of the sauna for the next two hours, sweating profusely and then cooling off in the cold shower in the courtyard where the snow melted around my feet as I walked. I bathed a final time in the cold waters of the cement bath, submerging myself completely and holding my breath as long as I could. There was an electric familiarity submerged in that icy water and I held myself beneath the surface as long as I could. I fought the urge to satisfy my body's desire for air until my world began to go dark and slowly I could make out music amid the faint tinny cackle of a car radio before my body was jolted to life and my face broke the surface of the water with gasps which echoed off the warm tiled walls of the sauna. I climbed out of the bath with the pounding of my heart in my ears and sat there on my knees until I had the strength to lift my body and walk back to the empty change room.

When I opened my locker there was a folded piece of paper with a name and address on it and a price in Euros and instructions to be on a park bench near the Zion Church in two days with a deposit. I folded the note and got dressed. I dressed slowly and walked out of the building into the street. I was calm and relaxed and the cold air felt nice. I walked down the sidewalks with my hands in my pocket, then entered the bar near the park. It was a long bar with wooden tables and chairs and the air was filled with the smoke from men who sat alone at the tables smoking. A single chandelier hung from a chain and on the square tables sat ashtrays and small candles which flickered inside small glass enclosures. Around a couple of tables were old plush chairs, the kind that invited small groups of drinkers and smokers but at each of these tables there was nobody. The bartender was thin, with a moustache, and he sat on a barstool behind the bar and suggested a wine when I ordered one and said nothing when he put it on my table at the back of the bar. Next to my table were two doors with *herren* and *damen* stencilled on them in paint that looked decades old. There were small lamps on a few of the tables and at the end of the bar a man sat ashing his cigarette to the beat of the old three-chord surf songs coming through the small speakers. In an exposed storage area above the bathroom doors was a poorly decorated Christmas tree, as though decorated once years ago and hauled out every year. I sat at my table near the washrooms and studied the patrons until I figured out who the dealer was. It didn't take long. I had a nose for these things. Every user does.

That night I dreamt I was waist high in a still river until I neared the fork where water from a much wider branch flowed quickly downstream. There were broken tree-branches in the water and when I reached my arm in to pull one out, the river dried up before my eyes, and the water was gone, entirely altered by such a small disturbance. I placed the branch back down and the riverbed was filled again as water cascaded violently down the hillside between jagged rocks. I rushed to the bank and was this time in deep snow. Upriver, atop the snow-draped cliffs I saw two wolves looking down at me, and halfway up the banks I could see a mountain lion perched on an outcropping. I lumbered through the snow in fear one or the other would make a move on me but the animals never moved. They just stood over me watching as a body floated past me in the river, carried face-down by the current, in a green military jacket stained with blood and three holes in the back.

7.

Berlin. December 25th.

Outside my window, the wind was blowing through the trees pulling frail leaves from the branches and it had been quiet enough that I could faintly hear the leaves landing delicately on the ground. I moved to the bedroom facing the courtyard and opened the window. It was cold but I wanted the air. I pulled the blankets over me as I lay there fully clothed in the bed and listened to the rain hitting the trees and the stones in the garden of the closed-in courtyard which stretched five storeys high on four sides and held the sound like a drum. But soon the rain stopped and widened into snowflakes.

Beneath the thin layer of snow were the carcasses of two pigeon hatchlings I'd found on the windowsill of the bathroom during late summer. I'd been excited about them, keen to see them one day take flight for the first time and to soar above the walled-in courtyard and see the world open up for them for the first time and I imagined how it would make them fly harder and higher. But that day never came. I'd left oat flakes and pieces of a baguette outside the window but days later there was one less bird in the nest and when I went to the courtyard to see where it had fallen and to see if it could be saved it was dead, its limp neck on the rim of a bicycle wheel locked to a grate beneath the window. I'd made a point not to open the window again in case the attention I'd paid the birds had caused the mother to react defensively. I had taken it as a personal message. This was the most intimate contact I'd had with any creature since arriving here. I was the only witness to the pigeon and her young. I'd opened the window that morning and seen her, beautiful and plump, and she looked at me and then reluctantly flew away exposing two pathetic dark and barely feathered young. That was the day I'd laid the oat flakes and crumbled baguette I'd taken from the cupboard. Days after, promising myself I would not open the window I couldn't help it but to check again. If the mother had abandoned the second one then maybe I could save it. But when I opened the window the remaining bird was dead, suffocated beneath the weight of its mother, and I felt a stupid sadness and guilt that week, as though my own actions had caused the deaths of these two young birds. I told myself it was dumb to feel bad, and that it wasn't because of anything I'd done, but I couldn't shake the gut feeling that I'd been responsible for the death of these creatures. It's a curious defence mechanism of birds, to murder their young when they've come too close to humans. It's a wonder there are any birds at all.

It was impossible to sleep. From the front window in the other room I'd heard an awful wail which sounded like the voice of a woman and I got up from the bed and went to the balcony but as the sound grew louder and the grinding of metal became more apparent I saw it was just a woman riding an old bicycle bent out of shape with a rim grinding against a wet wheel. I put on my jacket and walked to the tram station and rode the tram down to Alexanderplatz where I waited for the first train. It was an eastbound train and when it arrived it was mostly empty. I took a seat at the back and pressed my head against the window and stayed on until the last stop in a place called Ahrensfelde. There wasn't much to the place but over the houses I could make out a fleet of giant wind turbines. I'd set out towards them and as the spaces between the houses widened the field opened up and I was soon among these giant turbines spinning heavily and slowly in the early morning wind. There was enough sun to keep my face warm and I walked on the footpath with my hands in my pockets and paused when I saw around a dozen small deer gathered in the field between the turbines. I stood motionless, just staring, but when they took notice of me they quickly moved on. On the horizon I could see the TV tower at Alexanderplatz from where I'd caught the train and it was tiny on the horizon but I used it as a reference point to walk back to Berlin. My ankles and knees and back ached and I knew I'd be asleep as soon as my head hit the pillow. I walked until I found a bus stop but after half an hour of waiting and shivering nothing came and I continued walking. I walked through a cemetery in Weissensee and then around the small lake of the same name until I finally found a tram. My eyes closed with my head against the window and I woke up where I had started at Alexanderplatz. I got out to switch trams, to take the one that would take me back to my flat but in my exhaustion, or in my delirium, or in my insomnia, that was when I saw her. But it doesn't matter how fast you run. You'll never catch a ghost. They only catch you. I saw her through a crowd, and we stood there with our eyes locked, until the doors of a train opened and she was gone.

When I finally got back to the flat, I cupped water from the tap into my mouth, then undressed as I walked to the bedroom. I went to sleep and thought nothing more of the pigeons or deer and only of Syringa. In the bedroom the long white drapes were as still as the snow beneath the turbines in the fields of Ahrensfelde. I closed my eyes and dreamt of Syringa.

She was swimming beneath the giant rib-vaulted ceiling of the bath-house pool. On each side of her, arched colonnades veiled long arcades which stretched the length of the pool, and above her cavernous galleries extended to the high clerestory windows. Entirely alone in the pool, this place was her basilica, and she alone swam in the calm waters of the pool, the windows black above her. She was a swimmer, which is to say, there was a grace to her stroke, showing years of experience, in youth races or confidently in the open waters or lakes or seas as an adult. She powered through each stroke pulling herself across the surface and then her body disappeared as she swam along the pool's tiled floor. She exhaled deeply through her nose as her stretched torso grazed the surface of the pool floor. She dove a few more times beneath the surface, and when she surfaced at the far end of the pool, she took a look around the empty pool one more time to make sure she was alone. She turned her eyes to the upper gallery surrounding the pool and seeing it also empty, she lowered her bathing suit, first sliding her arms out of the shoulder straps, then rolling the suit to her waist and then down her legs, lifting each one out until she was naked in the water. She pushed with both legs off the tiled wall of the pool and plunged again, her body moving underwater as though she'd been born there, holding deeper and deeper breaths beneath the surface. She was underwater for what seemed like minutes, then emerged near the edge of the pool where she'd left her bathing suit, and resumed swimming with a quiet breast stroke with her head above water. Suddenly, in the dream, I was also underwater and she swam next to me but we were no longer in the pool. We were in the city and she was a giant, and the earth was flooded so high that when she swam it was high above the skyscrapers and with the force of each kick the buildings came apart from the top floors, slowly crumbling to the earth until it was just her, swimming above the rubble of a city she'd destroyed without even touching. We were then back in the pool, and she slowed her stroke as she reached the end of the pool and I felt the water on my chest as her eyes met mine. She walked towards me, the water slowly moving around her ribs and her arms, and then she reached out her two hands and held my face in her palms as she ran her fingers gently along the bridge of my nose and my cheeks the way a blind person sees a face. Her lips parted as she was about to speak but I looked down and saw we were up to our necks in blood.

8.

Berlin. December 31ˢᵗ. 11:30am

On my last day alive, I dressed in slacks and a collared shirt and kept the sleeves pulled down and went for breakfast at the empty café. There were wooden tables and chairs and a small sign and the whole place probably belonged more on a coastal fishing village that rarely gets the crowds. In the corner a woman sat writing into a notebook and paused to put on a thin wool cardigan before sipping her coffee and returning to her writing. The whole damn place smelled of cheese and it was coming from the plate on the writing woman's table. I sat spooning coffee into my mouth and heard the sound again of that click click click of heels on the street and I moved quickly outside foolishly believing for minute that it was Syringa. I took my coffee and the small glass of water from inside and sat at one of the small empty tables outside. Across the street was a typical five-storey apartment complex, a guitar shop, and an old shop overflowing with toys. I closed my eyes and swished the water slowly inside my mouth and between my teeth until the water was warm and I was suddenly in the onsen outside Kobe and I was with her for the second last time before they took her away.

9

Kyoto, Japan. 3 years earlier.

I missed Kyoto. It was a place I went back to often in my mind. It was seven years after the bomb at the disco when everything went south and nothing was the same again. We'd lost touch, checking in with each other around once a year. A happy birthday here or there but nothing more than that. I did my best to keep up with her or keep track of her but it became harder and harder once she finished the foreign service exam. As a journalist publishing stories regularly, I was much easier to find, and it was my job to stay visible, though I never guessed she'd ever kept tabs on what I was doing. It was a surprise then to find a message in my inbox that we were in the same country where I was on assignment to cover a summit in Tokyo. On the last day of the summit there was a train ticket waiting for me at the hotel to travel to Kyoto. I had no idea what to expect when I got off the train. But she was there, standing on the platform, in large brown sunglasses and her hair pulled back in a loose ponytail under a wide-brimmed hat. I wanted to give her a hug but she extended her hand to shake mine and, when I took it, I could feel her hand trembling and she gave me a pursed smile and wiped a tear from beneath her sunglasses with her other hand. I pulled her closer to hug her and I knew she could feel me shaking too. She immediately led me to another platform and we took a one-hour train to Nara. She stopped at a vending machine on the platform and bought two large cans of beer for the ride. We loosened up on the train, made small talk. In Nara, we walked among the tourists in the temples and the countless deer outside. She curled her arm around mine as we walked among the deer which occasionally nudged us looking for food. There was something strange and utopic about it all. The entire grounds, the temple, and lawns, were our stage before the backdrop of a massive Golden Buddha where we played the role of lovers in a far-off land before the wandering deer and tourists. But it was a version of us that only existed somewhere in a far-off universe. There was an ease in walking with her with her arm around mine. She'd married, had a child and lost one, and was spare in the details and I didn't push her for them. She asked if I'd married and I told her I had ten wives and forty children with more on the way and she told me she wasn't surprised. We left the park as our hunger grew and she led the way to the train station where I took two more beers from the vending machine as we headed for Kobe an hour away. I wasn't sure why we needed to go to three cities in one day but I didn't ask. We walked, this time with our arms closely around each other, and found a restaurant in the well-lit narrow streets of an historic district and spoke with our faces barely apart at our low-lit table over a mix of warm sake and cold beers. We kept the conversation light, each sure not to veer off the road of where the night was going. We paid the bill and weren't outside five seconds before our arms were around each other. We said nothing in the taxi. I felt her lips on my neck and her head on my shoulders as we rode in the taxi. She gave the driver instructions in Japanese and paid in cash when we arrived at the Arima hotel and onsen. The onsen staff bowed courteously as she pulled me past reception. The halls were dimly lit and the walls lined with bamboo and rice paper. She walked me up to the room, and slid open the doors. There was no bed in the room, just two tatami mats on the floor side by side with thin bedding on top. I walked to the window as she lit a candle on the low table. The room was a place outside of time. It could have been a hundred or five hundred years ago. I walked to the window and looked outside but could make out little in the darkness. When I turned around she was standing naked, bathed in moonlight beside the bed on the floor.

In the morning we ate in the dining area, I in a loose yukata, and she in her kimono and I whispered to her that I felt like a samurai and she smiled and we ate small pieces of fish cooked over a tea light. I hardly knew what the other items on the tray were but she pointed them out and what order they were to be eaten and with what and I followed suit. Her kimono had become loose above the waist and when she leaned forward I could see the top of her breast and it made me hungrier. After breakfast we soaked naked in the powerful ferruginous waters of the onsen overlooking Mount Rokko. The men were separated from the women and I sat silent in the hot pools among the men and cooled off by pouring small pails of cold water over my naked body. But when I dressed back into my yukata, closing it one side over the other before tying it closed, a man stopped me and told me I had closed the robe the wrong way. "You must do other side first," he told me. "Only dead man wear robe this way."

I thanked him and closed the robe properly, then returned to the room. It was empty and I feared Syringa had gone. But she arrived shortly after with a warm bottle of sake which we drank on the two tatami mats on the floor. We barely spoke. She opened my robe, and I hers, and when I was inside her, here at the foot of Mount Rokko, I felt like this mountain was my home and I'd returned after a thousand years.

We soaked in the onsen one more time before leaving the next day and when we met in our room I was sitting half-dressed in my street clothes in the natural light and plucking quietly at the strings of the small toy guitar we'd picked up at a night kiosk in the market in Kobe after the restaurant and she looked out the window once and then back to me and pulled the wooden hairpin from her hair which fell behind her shoulders and then opened her kimono and when she did it was night all over again.

When we left the onsen after sunset I raised my arm for a taxi but
she held it down and we hurried across the street into an Ameri-
can-style hotel and stayed there for one more night never leaving
the room once. She hurried into the hotel and frequently looked
over her shoulder as we checked in and when we walked down
the hall towards our room. The bathrobes lacked the charm
of the traditional robes at Arima and she said they made her
feel like an old woman so she spent the day in one of my long-
sleeved shirts and nestled her legs under the blanket or under
my legs when she got cold. We ordered drinks up to our room
and we laughed or spoke or were just silent. She kept me inside
of her until it was no longer possible to do so without pain and
still we continued. She peed with the door open. Showered with
the door open and later in the evening, when she found blood
on my shirt that she'd been wearing, she had new clothes sent up
from the boutique downstairs. I said it was not a problem, and
that I had other shirts, but she had one sent up anyway.

In the middle of the night I woke and she was sitting by the window. I didn't know why she was sitting there, and I decided to
leave her alone. However, it was clear the next day that we were
being followed and that she had known this. That maybe she had
seen them in the car behind the taxi and pressed my arm down
when I had lifted it and had me jog with her around the corner
into this hotel. Or maybe not, and I hoped for the latter possibil-
ity. That maybe she just didn't want this affair to end yet and only
after we checked in did she discover we were being followed.
And maybe this explained the tears in her eyes when she was on
top of me, the ones she buried in my neck when she saw that I'd
seen them, the ones that made her press her body harder into
mine, squeezing her hips together and moving on top of me like
a swimmer against the current, holding my head down as she
breathed through snotty nose and even in my neck I could feel
the difference between sweat and tears and when I finally saw

her face I could see both and her hair was across her face and wet with both and there was no sound in the room but the breathing of us both.

I found the printed ticket by the bed in the morning and a new suit by the new shirts she'd had sent up the night before. I searched for my shirt she'd worn and bled on and there was nothing I wanted more at that moment than that shirt but it was gone. The ticket was a one-way from Kyoto to Tokyo and there was money with the word "taxis" written on one of the bills. I took a taxi to Kobe and walked through a thick market and when I got to the other side I took another taxi to the train station and travelled to Kyoto. It soon became clear I was being followed, regardless of how evasive I tried to be. In the station I acted normally while keeping my eyes on the men watching me from the other seats in the wagon. I wore sunglasses even though it was grey and overcast and this allowed me to stare at them and study them as they tried not to appear as though they were following me.

I watched the towns outside the window buzz by and kept waiting for a patch of open uninhabited land to break the landscape but it never did. It almost never does in central Japan. All towns bleed into the next. I saw the same men in the airport and they were less guarded about going unnoticed and when I passed the gate to board the plane I turned and there were two of them standing shoulder to shoulder watching me as I made my way down the long boarding tunnel.

I held the vision of her in my mind as long as I could and fought in my mind to go back to the onsen but I couldn't and when I opened my eyes I was sitting back outside the small café in Berlin. I walked into the small guitar shop across the street. The shop was half workshop half shop and a punk-looking woman with an apron on behind a desk scattered with tools mumbled hello as I walked slowly in front of the guitars on the wall, thumbing the odd string. By the exit sat a basket filled with cheap ukuleles and one of them looked like the small toy guitar from Kobe. I ran my fingers along the neck and body and I could see my hand shaking. I pulled my hand from the instrument, and pushed the door open, ringing the small bell above. I walked until I reached the Zion Church and drank on a bench beneath the spire at the back. I would never learn what she had gotten into in Japan that attracted that kind of attention. All that was clear was she was flying close to the sun and had taken great care to make sure it was me that didn't get burned. I smoked cigarettes until my throat hurt and I felt sick and when there was nothing left to drink and nothing left to smoke I stumbled back to my flat.

"So you left."

I could hear Hissel's voice as I lay in the bed. He was so much a part of me, he didn't need to be there for me to hear his voice.

"Yes."

"You never tried to find her."

"No. It was to protect her. If I'd led them —"

"Please. You're not on trial."

"A woman whose job it is to be unseen disappears in Japan and I'm supposed to know where to find her?"

"Okay," Hissel said. "But think. Is there a place you would have looked? If you'd stayed. I mean if you had to look anywhere."

"Yes, probably."

"Where?"

"The river. Near the hotel. There's a place in the river in Kyoto with the carved stones jutting out for people to cross. I would have looked there."

"But you didn't."

"The train ticket was for Tokyo. I assumed it was a sign to leave. To go there and board a plane and leave. We'd never spent any time in Tokyo. There is no place I could have looked."

"Maybe the train ticket was a choice."

"Then I guess I underestimated her."

"Or you underestimated her love for you."

"Maybe."

"Do you miss her?" he asked.

It was a stupid question.

"I miss sleeping beside her with my face in her hair. I miss the way she cooked everything from scratch and left nothing on the bone when she was finished eating and the way she sat at the table with her knees pulled to her chest. I miss the way she'd drive with her long tanned bare feet on the gas pedal as we drove through the countryside. I miss the taste of her mouth. Her voice that sounded like a cello when she hummed when she thought she was alone. I miss everything. Everything."

10

Berlin. November 17

"Why did you go after her?"

It was Hissel's voice again but this time he was sitting beside me on the bench outside the Zion Church as trams rumbled past us. Once upon a time, the Zion Church, or *Zionkirche* had been at the centre of political opposition to the GDR, doubling as a church, and an underground printing press and punk rock venue once famously stormed by skinheads under the watchful eye of state police. For now it was just a nice church on a hill in a nice neighbourhood.

"Because I wanted it to be her."

"What you would have said?"

"I don't know. That I looked for her. That I tried everything to find her. That I never gave up for a second. That I never stopped searching. That I am always searching."

"What did you do for her the moments she was taken?"

"I was in handcuffs with a knee in the back of my neck."

"Like her."

"I'm only here to give you money, Hissel. Just take it."

"You don't like your fixer here in Berlin."

"You're no fixer, Hissel."

"You're no contractor. Why don't you do this yourself?"

"Because this can't be the last thing I fuck up."

"Okay ghosthunter, well is already half wrong."

"What do you mean?"

"You got your second name wrong."

"How do you know?"

"Second name is wrong. The one who would not help you. First name good. He gave the order to detain her. The second name is man who wouldn't help you."

"How do you know? I have a photo."

"I know your photo. Refugee football match. Name on photo is wrong."

"Give me the name then."

"I'll need the first half next week. Things cost money."

"It doesn't work like that. I gave you a list. You have the names."

"Was wrong names."

"Well now you have the right names."

"My man bring you right name, the *right* name of man who refuse to help you. When you look it up you see where he is. My contact is good contact. Your contact …"

He gestured by waving his hand in front of his face. It's a thing Germans do. An unsubtle way to signal that they think you're crazy. Feign catatonic and wave a hand in front of two dumb-looking eyes.

I got up from the bench and started to walk away.

"Why do you remember things the way you do?" he said. "You have a choice. Why do you let the sound of her wailing stick in your ear more than the sound of her breath as she slept beside you and where you slept with your face in her soft hair? Why with a lifetime ahead of you to store memories you make no space in your mind for her cheek against your cheek. You remember falling bombs, not tissue paper butterflies in the air at a concert where you found each other in the crowd of a hundred thousand people? You taste nothing but the bitterness of a few nights gone wrong, you let the salt on skin after evening swims in the sea disappear into the ether … for what? Let her go."

I stood with my back to Hissel. I wanted to punch him. I wanted to climb on top of him, choke him into lifelessness, and smash his face into the ground and see his blood run through the small stones but I was choking back the tears and I didn't want him to see that I knew that he was right so I raised my hand in a half-wave, said goodbye, and started walking again.

"Why you walk away? You busy man. Maybe you have place to go. Chase down ghosts on another train. Maybe … to make fire in basement of girl's dormitory in laundry room in middle of the night?"

I turned around to face him. "What did you say?"

He clicked his dentures, then stuck them out at me, the kind of grotesque move an old uncle makes to scare the kids when no one else is looking. There'd been a fire in a girl's dorm. That much was reported. But that was all that was reported. It was Syringa who told me the fire had been started in the laundry room beneath their dorms in the middle of the night, and not in the morning as the girls dressed, as the papers had reported it. They burned in their locked bedrooms, and the fire killed them all by morning.

11.

Hissel was in my head and he knew it. I needed to follow him, get him to lead me somewhere. To his contact. To his home. Anywhere. I was ill. My kidneys ached and I'd started pissing blood and he probably sensed my desperation. He kept asking to meet even though there was no need and when we met, my answers to his questions were short. He was making me paranoid. If it was his plan, it worked. But I still tried to be cool, to come off less unhinged. I agreed to another meeting with him and told him I'd have the first half of the deposit. It wasn't much. A few thousand Euros. He had a sense of humour about it and gave me half the letters of the second name I needed in no order so I told him to go fuck himself and left. I found a place where I could watch him on the bench and follow him when he finally left. He sat there for some time and behind his sunglasses it was impossible to tell if he was staring ahead or sleeping. After about thirty minutes he rose from the bench and walked into the swell of people coming up the stairs of the underground U-Bahn station. I followed not far behind and moved quickly down the stairs but when I got to the platform he was nowhere to be seen so I boarded the train on the long shot he was on it. I made my way through the wagons as they lurched around corners, dipping below street level and then shooting out of the tunnels and climbing the high iron bridges over the streets but after a half dozen stops, changing train cars and quickly scouring the platforms, I gave in to the fact that he'd given me the slip. And why shouldn't he? He'd given NATO the slip. And Afghanistan the slip. He'd given half of Europe the slip. Why should I be any different? I walked up the stairs of the last

U-Bahn station, put my hands in my pockets and buried my face in the collar of my coat.

Soon it was me arranging to meet him again. I told him the money was getting hard to come by and I could only give him small amounts at a time. He never took issue with it. It was always the same scene. We'd sit somewhere. Chat a little. He never rushed me to leave or got up first. Each time I'd try to follow him but he made it hard by never leaving first. He could sit for hours beside me, with our faces to the sun or to the clouds and never move, even if he was shivering and clearly cold. Once we sat on a bench by a canal near a Turkish market filled with locals and tourists. We were alone on the bench until an old woman sat beside us and Hissel moved closer to me. They spoke briefly. Small talk. The weather. And when the woman left Hissel stayed where he was close beside me and never spoke. I didn't move either. It was my plan to out-wait him so I could follow him when I left. I stared straight across the canal to the market. I could hear the men hollering deals from the fruit and vegetable stands through the buzz of market-goers and when it started to drizzle rain, there were fewer people walking by, fewer cyclists gliding past, and I felt Hissel's head on my shoulder. I didn't know if he was awake or asleep, I didn't know if he was tired, or just fucking with me. So I sat there. In silence. I closed my eyes and listened to the muffled voices from across the river or the pebbles beneath the wheels of cyclists passing by us. I listened for his breath but heard nothing. He was like a ghost. A heavy ethereal presence. Like a memory that weighs you down so bad your shoulders hunch and your knees ache. Or one that draws you out to sea and then drowns you. When he woke it was with a hard jolt and he was sitting straight up.

"Go. I go now."

He put his hand on my leg and pushed himself up then walked quickly toward the U-Bahn station where I followed him.

When we met that day, I had come with a backpack. Every time we'd met when I was trying to tail him I had it. I kept a baseball cap and a black windbreaker inside it. I put both on and stuffed the backpack into a garbage bin outside the station. I stayed one car back so I could see him through the window of the train wagon, and I followed him almost to the last station. There were so few people on the train now that I thought he would make me for sure. I stayed in the wagon and out of sight, on a hard gamble that the doors would close or I would lose him as he left the station. When the platform was empty I left and the doors closed behind me. I walked quietly out of the station and was able to keep him in my sights. He walked a few hundred metres then turned into a *schrebergarten* commune. When he entered the gate I picked up my pace until I also reached the entrance. He was about fifty metres up the narrow path with the trees hanging over the fences of the garden plots. But when I opened the gate, and the latch dropped, he turned around, paused for a moment at the top of the path. And then he was gone. I hurried up the path, first walking and then running. The whole area was silent. The cottages were mostly used by locals in the summertime so there was no one around. The path was made even more narrow by the branches of overhanging lilac trees. They were everywhere and their dead flowers hung from the branches and I could still make out the mild smell of rot which hung lightly in the air. My run slowed to a walk. The path curled around and finally spit me out where I'd come in. It was possible he'd known I was on to him and he led me here just to lose me. I wandered up and down the path, peering over the fences and into the windows of the small houses. If he'd been inside of one, staring through the cracks in a curtain — then he'd have made me for sure.

On the train back to my flat I went over Hissel's choppy version of his story in my head. The story that he'd been detailed to transport a prisoner but somewhere along the way they both went missing. It was a story full of strange details and large holes. I'd tried searching but info was absolutely airtight on prisoner movement, so it was his story or nothing. There was no way he'd transported a prisoner alone so if his story was true, then whoever had accompanied him on that transport was probably dead. He said knowing what he'd been told by the prisoner, on top of what he had done, a criminal charge was the least of his worries and being caught would cost him far more than his job as a soldier. He had escaped that night with the prisoner by stealing a car which they drove for hours through the night until it ran out of gas. He grew his beard, travelled carefully, and eventually stowed away across the Caspian to Azerbaijan. But the only plausible route to Azerbaijan was from a port city in Turkmenistan and if he'd somehow regrouped and made his way to Georgia, as he said he had, then there was over a thousand-kilometre gap between that car running out of gas and that beard growing that he was leaving out.

"You know what I did in Georgia? Huh? I ski! I ski and I eat." There was a short pause. "I eat and eat." He laughed at this and he was right that the thought of a German NATO defector on top of a Georgian ski slope was comical, especially given the trip into Europe, if across land, would be another three thousand kilometres and involve crossing either Turkey or two borders of Russia. But both ways were possible. Entering Europe by land was by no means impossible, and by his account he'd stolen cars, hitched rides on trucks, motorbikes, even the odd horse, and paid bribes to get him across borders through the trunks of cars and into the cargo holds of container ships or long-distance trains. It wasn't hard to imagine him, standing on top of a Georgian ski slope staring west, or riding in the cab of a truck with the sun in his face crossing the arid and mountainous valleys of the easternmost parts of Europe. Eventually, he made it to Berlin, doing it all just to live right under their noses, walking across the lawns of the Reichstag every day to remind himself how close he could get to people now. He told me how he'd even gone in once with a large group of tourists with his name on the visitors' ledger hoping it would ring the right bells and staring down at them from the top of the glass dome above the Reichstag, he knew it was probably the wrong move to try and smoke people out of their holes with the knowledge that he was close and that he knew things which would torpedo the lives of very powerful people. He could see security scramble below from the observation but when they came up the elevators and rounded the stairs in the glass dome he was gone. But now they knew he was here. Knew that he was right under their noses and ready to go off. By emerging once out of his hole he'd sent those who knew what he knew into a cover from which they would not emerge but through bulletproof escort. What he would never tell me is that we were looking for the same people.

I asked him if he enjoyed the skiing in Georgia. He smiled and then touched my knee. "Was okay. But really I wanted beach. Not a ski-man. Beach-man. You like beach?"

"Yes I like beach," I said.

"Of course you like beach. Pretty girls at beach ... You have wife?"

"No."

"Why not? You lose one girl you take another. Have happy life."

"It didn't work like that for me."

That day by the canal in summer, the day we first met, when he
first let on about a story involving a prisoner, he just sat there
staring into the water. I asked him if he had a job and he shook
his head, still staring straight ahead. We shared a few beers on a
bench and talked a bit more and occasionally he would touch my
leg or hold my elbow when he was telling me something. After
a while, and a couple more runs to the shop for beers, we were
both drunk, or at least I was drunk, and the conversation drifted.
When the sun finally set, I let him know that I knew about a job.
An ex-soldier's kind of job, I told him. Work he might be good
at or someone he knows might be good at. He was quiet and listened as I explained that time was an issue and he sensed the ur-
gency in my voice. "There's money," I said. "Lots of money." This
part was half true. There was what was left from two inheritances
and a family cottage, as well as what I'd saved from writing from
back when writing was something you could live off. I'd sold
everything I owned in Canada before I came here. Every meaningless and meaningful item or piece of furniture. My grandfa-
ther's piano I'd kept in a cottage outside of Kingston, and later
the cottage itself. I kept most of the cash in a black leather bag in
my flat. I wasn't planning on dying with anything to my name, I
spent little, of what I did, most went to cheap rent I paid in cash
and a bit of food. The rest went into my arm, and even then I was
economic about that.

"I am easy to find. Come here at lunch time on a Saturday. I know
your face now."

"Will you be here?"

"You won't see me at first," he said. "But come here. I know your
face now. Then walk on. Do your day. I will find you."

"Okay," I said, and I stood up slowly. We didn't shake hands or say goodbye but as I walked away he spoke.

"Was woman —" he said. I turned around and he repeated the words. "Was woman."

Two words. And then a third, that bound him forever to me that day.

"Who was woman?" I asked.

"Prisoner. Was woman."

12.

Berlin. November 22

I couldn't get Hissel's words out of my head. I took a shower and dressed, and when I went out, I passed a bakery, paying the 35 cents needed for a small bun. There was a short line, and in front of me small kid held a list she'd been given by her parents and some coins clutched in her small palm. When she got to the front of the line, she read off the list as the woman behind the counter listened patiently, filling the brown paper bag with the different breads the girl named. She smiled at the girl when she finished her order, took her money and returned her change. When the girl left, it was my turn and the woman turned to me and smiled mechanically as I pointed to the single roll that I wanted. It was enough to fill my stomach, the days long gone now of desiring any food beyond what minimally sustained me. It hadn't always been like this. There had once been a life were breakfast stretched into lunch and lunch stretched into dinner. There had long ago been a life with walks to the bakeries or supermarkets in whatever clothes were on the floor next to the bed to get eggs and bread to fry together breakfast for the two of us to eat, Syringa draped in T-shirt or tank top on warm days or in winter when she sat with her entire body beneath an oversized sweater or hoodie. There had once been a time when the writing was on the wall that this charade was unsustainable but the letters were so big, and the light so blinding, it was impossible to read.

I took the thirty-five-cent roll from the bag and broke it into pieces as I walked. I walked to empty my mind but it didn't work so I kept on walking to burn myself out through exhaustion, until the very act of walking shot a pain through my ankles, knees,

and hips that made the anguish moot. After hours of wandering
the city, I rounded a corner where a tram came to a loud slow
stop. The streets were wet, and the sun was setting as though
it hadn't even tried to rise. That time of year a six-month cloud
hung over most of the country, and everything from the streets
to the bones were permanently damp and cold. On the wet
streets, walled on each side by the five-storey buildings which
curved over the embedded tram tracks, the light from street
lamps and traffic lights speckled and curled along each side of the
steel tracks. I crossed the street as a tram approached and then
slowed to a stop. I made nothing of the people filing out of the
tram. Some trudged out slowly, burying their faces in the collars
of their jackets or scarves, and a few others passed me, including
one with a gait that said get me home, get me under a blanket
or get me to my lover to inundate these streets with the waters
that open only in the first months of love. But one more person
lingered or passed and I was suddenly in the haze of cheap cig-
arillo smoke that like a cruel time machine catapulted me back
to what felt like a hundred years ago to when Syringa and I were
teenagers. I kept my pace and let the smoke hang over me and
transport me and there I was, suddenly back in our hometown
where we'd scoped out the bars that let us in underage and where
we then became regulars. I'd had a fake ID we'd made one night
in her parents' basement but she'd never needed one because
even at seventeen she had a beauty that felt alien to turn away
at the door. On weekends we went to a pub which filled up with
university students to hear an old Irish man sing a mixed bag of
Irish, American, or Acadian folk songs. The students in the bar
were twenty-one or twenty-two but felt like full-blown adults to
us. They sang along to songs about this or that Mary or Sue from
Dublin or Halifax in 1778 or 1916 as though the music were history's sloshing wine and they were its goblet. At seventeen, we
thought this is what adulthood must be like, hoisting beers and
singing out loud to honour men or women romantically felled in

storms or Irish towns while the snow fell slowly outside the window of a bar in our small meaningless town. We dressed the way the students dressed, trading in our ripped and frayed jeans and faded black band shirts for deck shoes, proper slacks, and thick wool sweaters we wore with collared shirts underneath. We'd raid the thrift stores for preppy looking clothes that made us look like twenty-something university students. For fun, when we were drunk she would challenge me to pick up a university girl. I'd tell them my major was marine biology, a poor tell in a landlocked school that specialized in engineering and economics and where the closest marine mammal was a captive orca in a theme park four hundred kilometres away where they underfed the animals so they'd hurriedly approach the park-goers as though it was fondness and not starvation that motivated them to do so. The pickup game in the pub was a one-player game because she would have won every time — for fun she'd choose the dumb girl — her words — to fall for my marine biology line and when I came back numberless and shrugging, she'd share the loss with me and we'd drink more until the bar slowly filled up as the singer went into another crowd favourite. At times, few that they were, that the line did work, I would cozy up to the university girl, and always look back to Syringa, for what looked like approval but what was really just projection. When I ran my fingers along the bare arm of the girl it was really along Syringa's arm. When caught up in the moment, going nose to nose and then lips to lips with a stranger, I would look her way, and she would know it was her lips I wanted to taste. She never budged, never got jealous, or at least never appeared to, she just kept her eyes on mine and smiled, knowing I couldn't sustain the seduction forever, because as soon as someone approached her as she sat alone, I'd come rushing back.

She'd had a boyfriend that year, a second-year philosophy student who could make her feel smart one moment and then small

the next. Their relationship wasn't mine to understand. We were
both seventeen, but she felt years older. The first time she ever
kissed me we'd been at that pub, with our beers in the air like we
were old the way twenty-one-year-olds are old when you're seventeen and sang along to the songs. The bar closed and the snow
began to fall and we walked out of the pub together. She'd asked
me to walk her to her boyfriend's dorm before catching — if I
was lucky — the last bus home. But the snow was everywhere
and coming down hard and there were no busses or cabs in sight.
We trudged through the snow together as it crunched beneath
our feet — I don't know what we talked about — nothing and
everything — but as we walked the temperature dropped by
what felt like degrees per minute. She clung firmly to my arm
and buried her face in my collar as we walked and when we were
near her boyfriend's dorm and stared down the street looking
for a cab, every cab that passed us was full. I told her I'd walk — it
wasn't a far walk — a few kilometres — and we were both drunk
enough for the distance not to matter or compute but at that
moment the cold was real and all around us and as I hugged her
goodbye we held on a little longer just to feel the warmth of each
other's bodies and she asked then as her face was against mine
if I would miss her when she left. I didn't know what she meant
and just to taunt her I said no — no — I wouldn't miss her and
she leaned back and glared, squinting her eyes and furrowing her
eyebrows until I caved and told her what we both knew to be true
which was — yes — yes a galactic yes, yes I would fucking miss
her no matter where she went and it was then as the snow came
down all around us, melting on our noses and our cheeks as our
faces got closer and closer. At first it was just our noses touching
before we each opened our mouths and breathed in the night
and the city and the snow and the stars and I felt the warmth of
her mouth inside of mine. Like a junkie ravaging years off their
body chasing their first high, I was no different, but I was chasing
a galaxy of love in the mouth of a ghost.

I could almost taste the cherry-dipped plastic filter on my lips. I could still smell the smoke. It stuck to me, hung on to me until I finally shook it off by walking into the first café that came into view. I sat in the first seat I saw and I ordered red wine, and then another. The place was warm and with each drink I could feel my kidneys tighten. Red velvet cushions stapled into chairs and an Indian woman in the corner thumbed through a magazine with an empty glass of tea in front of her. My movements these days were predictable. If anyone were looking for me, I'd be an easy target. It was a late afternoon and I was staring straight ahead and a woman walked in and sat at the table beside me. I didn't turn to see her but I could make out a slender wrist in the corner of my eye and I let the scent of her perfume take over.

I closed my eyes briefly as she pointed to something on the menu and I inhaled deeply. It was a scent I knew and I closed my eyes again and held them shut and when I opened them again it was early morning and I'd just arrived in Manhattan where I would have twenty-two hours before I waved goodbye to Syringa as she left in a black SUV to go to the airport. I had never been to New York before that, and the whole thing had been done on a whim, a late-night telephone call to say she was back in town for a couple of days before she had to be in New York for a flight, and that she just wanted to hear my voice, and possibly see me, followed forty-eight hours later by a taxi ride to the bus station and the eight-hour drive to New York overnight so somehow extend that visit as long as was humanly possible. So I never learned any of the names and never went back and the whole thing was a con-flagration of textures and flavours and images which, feverishly against my will, fade as do dreams in the morning, until I am left with a handful of images I can barely piece together but it started with a picture of her standing outside an apartment on Rivard Street in Montreal where I was housesitting for a friend and where she was in town for a meeting and the early August air was cool as the rain came down and she was wearing a denim jacket and a long dress and holding an umbrella over her head and her suitcase and it was one day until she flew to New York and it was three days or so until I arrived at her hotel doorstep and we saw each other again and pretended like it was in the old days when we'd met in Montreal and she could just be herself, her old self, and walk around the city in her shitty sneakers as I showed her the new place to get Indian food and pretended to play it cool when inside I was negotiating with God a way to just stop time before she left and all God left me was enough bread in my pocket to get on a bus in the middle of the night. When I arrived she was there with a coffee waiting for me and I remember her tan dress with the printed feathers on it and her tan legs that would walk me up and down this island until our legs were too tired to take us any farther and by the time the coffee was done we were sitting in a diner and we shared a bagel and a cup of brewed coffee and an orange juice and when the bill finally came I paid and we left and rounded the corner and found an empty bench to sit down by some pond in Central Park where she put her arms around me and talked about this or that and we both bravely and silently acknowledged the impermanence of it all but the knowledge that she was leaving again and might never return prompted us to get up and walk as though fleeing from this fact so we could enter the abyss of this giant city that she knew so well and when we did the next thing I knew there was a black family singing in an underpass or hall in the park where their voices resonated off the bricks and made them sound bigger than they really were or maybe as big as they really were and before their voices settled she was buying me a cold drink and we were sitting in another park where there were steel chairs and small steel tables and I can't remember if this is before or after she took me into the public library to get away from the heat and as I stood there looking at all those books I thought there just weren't enough words in my language or in any language

anywhere that would ever describe her the way I saw her and
there were no words for the softness of her lips nor enough to
capture the million shades of emerald in the cobweb iris of her
eyes but I said none of this because it was the click click click of
her shoes against the stone steps as we left and ventured to the
centre of it all and then it was the click click click of her shoes
against the steps that lead to St. Michael's or St. Patrick's or St.
George's or St. Somebody's but wherever it was this place was
a sanctuary for me, uniquely out of place because outside there
were scores upon scores of people walking or running or buying
or stealing or selling or whatever it is they did out there but in
this church in this sanctuary there were less than a dozen people
and some were praying and some were just staring straight ahead
and I sat with her and it may not have been romantic except that
in my head I was playing make-believe and I was a believer and
this was our church and this was where we went for her to pray
for a way out and for me to pray to stop time until it was her
shoes again on the stony floor and the next thing I knew we were
next to water or a lake or the ocean but wherever we were it was
past the middle of the day and flowers were growing out of an
old railroad and there were no trains only people walking and
she was holding my face in her hands and telling me to kiss her
because this could be the last time and when I finally caught my
breath we were in a small French restaurant and she was breaking a pigeon or a quail egg over uncooked meat and I was sipping
a beer and I knew by the position of the sun that it would soon
be night but she was just getting started and there was more she
wanted to show me and there was the sound of the train and a
man preaching togetherness and I smiled at him and he smiled
back and he was probably a dime-a-dozen crazy man in this city
but he punched my fist or shook my hand I can't remember but
it doesn't matter because then we were near a university and we
were sitting again before we walked down to slap that giant bull
on its ass for luck and a way to relive the night she arrived under

the umbrella — the night we danced in my friend's apartment, that night when the two of us were young again for a moment but by now the sun was moving at an ungodly rate and darkness was coming upon us and the heavy cloud over us as I saw for the first time just how goddamn big this place was where two towers that stood as lovers over the city came crumbling down was somehow softened when I asked a man for directions on how to get out of here and she smiled and reminded me again that the men in the country where she worked now didn't ask for directions and I thought to myself that if I ever landed in there I would ask every man in that country how to find her only that's not necessary right now because for now, in this city, we had already found each other only the exhaustion was overcoming us and we were heavy legs on the subway platform somewhere in a place they call midtown where her hotel was and the next thing I knew we were eating empanadas very late at night in a Chilean restaurant because we were hungry after making love because our plans to go see the view from the top of this building or that building ended the minute she walked out of the shower wrapped in only a towel and I knew that the view from wherever could wait because a view like this, like the sun setting on the last day on earth, may never come around again and we went back to the hotel after the empanadas because no matter what this city had to offer there were only hours left of her and we made love once again and the next thing I knew it was a black SUV and we were sitting in the back and she dropped me off at the bus station on her way to the airport and she said I'll see you around or I'll see you next year or I'll see you back here in New York, but it would be three years before I saw her again, standing in large sunglasses on a train platform in Kyoto.

When I opened my eyes (were they even closed?) I was hyperventilating. I turned to see the woman beside me but she was facing the other way as I looked at her neckline. Her hair was down and covering her face as she faced the entrance to her right. I watched as she abruptly placed a few Euros on the table, rose and left, and I watched every single step she took as she exited the restaurant, rounded the corner, and then disappeared past the last window. I did my best to get a handle on my breathing, not to stick out, or draw attention. I soon calmed down and walked home slowly and when I arrived there was a manila envelope on the floor by the door. I opened it, and there were two large photos of two men and I could tell by the cream-coloured taxis and the yellow on the busses in the background of the photos that they were in Berlin.

Later, I looked up the name of the Irish singer from the bar in our hometown and saw that he was dead. He'd died of dementia, a mind wiped of any memory he had of any of those nights when the snow fell perfectly softly behind the windows, while inside the two of us would sing along to folk songs with beer splashing in our glasses, playing grown-up in a world slowly painting giant fucking targets over our hearts and our backs.

13

Berlin. December 1

"They broke her jaw with a shovel."

We were sitting outside a café near the Zionkirche again. It felt like weeks since the sun had been out. The trees were unspectacular around the church. But he kept his eyes on them when he spoke again.

"Most of teeth were gone. And this was after she was transferred from local police. They were worst. They delay her transfer and everyone knew why. But for them it was part of the process. Part of breaking her. Only ... it didn't work."

He'd finally found a gear to talk so I just sat and listened. As he spoke it was getting clear he'd helped a prisoner escape, but he didn't say how or who or why. Whatever happened, what he was describing was the night he went from being a soldier to something that transcends the very notion of the free man, for when he turned the key and led her out of the prisoner van he went from being soldier to a free man to a fugitive in a country where his own country would not shelter him nor help him and the moment he realized this he went from being a fugitive to a man without a state or legal existence, politically naked, sacred and accursed. That night they drove in a stolen car across the cold arid plains until it ran out of gas. When they woke in the morning, they were hypothermic, and surrounded by a Pashtun farmer or villager or herder, he wasn't sure, only that the man was with two young men he took to be his sons and the prisoner was ill and feverish with infection.

"They took us in. This man and his sons. It is the Pashtun way. He covered us in back of his car and sons put the stolen car into a ravine."

He didn't know exactly how long they'd stayed with the man or his sons or where they'd been hidden. He guessed it was a few weeks or more, enough for her to find her strength to move again, and when the prisoner was mostly healed, they were taken near the border with Uzbekistan with the city of Termez not far across the Amu River.

"We both knew we couldn't walk across the bridge. There were soldiers, and they would have killed us. So we waited. And we tried to cross the river alone at night."

"What happened to her?"

Hissel clicked his dentures a few times. Chewing on nothing. Just clicking those dentures against each other as though chewing on some indigestible account of the past.

"The water was so cold. The water from the Amu. It comes from a glacier. I was weak. She was weaker. I pulled her across, but we were spotted. Shots were fired and I was hit in the shoulder. When I fell she covered me with her body and then they shot three bullets into her. Whap, whap, whap. She wasn't dead but she was going to be soon. She pat me on back. Go, she told me. Go, go, go, go, go."

"So you left her?"

"No. I was so tired. And it was dark. They were shining lights but we were behind a rock."

"Then what happened?"

"Wait, she said. After she said go go go go go, she said wait!"

He clicked his dentures again, rat-tat-tat-tat-tat-tat.

"In the water, she told me. Put me in the river. So I slid her to river where it was deep and the water was moving fast. Her eyes widened when she felt the water again on her body. And then they closed. I held her face to mine to feel her breath but there was none. And so I let her go and the river took her away."

He was quiet after that and I said nothing in case there was more he would add to the story. He finally spoke again, while nodding at the trees across from us.

"These trees," Hissel said.

"The lilacs?"

"They are everywhere. Not native to Europe. They were a gift from Ottomans. Very beautiful. Resilient. They explode to life early. You can cut off their heads and they come back stronger. But they die early, and when they rot, they rot."

"Did you love her?"

"What difference it make?"

"Do you think she loved you?"

Hissel was silent for a while, before finally nodding.

"Yes. She love me very much."

14

Berlin. December 2

That night, after meeting Hissel, I dreamt of her again. We were by the bank of the St. Lawrence where the water meets the shores of Wolfe Island not far from where the car went through the ice when I was a child. In the dream, most of the houses had been erased by a storm. It was a tiny village on a hill by a lake. It had been levelled. A sliver of a house remained — completely intact two-floor section of the home with shutters and porch, bricks and shards of window — but the whole thing less than a metre wide on each side. It stood in the skeletal wood like a totem pole. She was distraught and I offered to bring her photos from the archives (what archives?) but when I unrolled the black and white aerial photo it was a different town from a different time and this made her more distraught. Farther ahead, at the edge of the clearing where the wood began, we found ourselves surrounded by a large swarm of bees oblivious to us. They were gathered on the path surrounding two other members of their swarm thrashing around on the path and kicking up flecks of earth and I couldn't tell if this was some fight to the death or a ritual copulation anticipated for generations somewhere in the scrolls of bees. To my right I saw a small turtle spinning forwards and sideways in its place, its head tucked into its shell and its limbs curled inwards — until it sprung bright yellow flower petals — as though in those seconds it had undergone millennia of evolutionary adaptation meant to blend it to its surroundings. I bent down and tried to take a photo with the camera in my hands but as it came into focus it reverted to its original form and the turtle slowly poked its head out of its shell and I was able to capture it in its dance. In the dream, I took a few more photos of the nearby lake and the rocky shore but when I showed them to her nothing was still. The images were alive in the viewfinder and the whole scene alive with vibrant light, capturing mist over the still lake as only a dream can.

The dream was immediately followed by another, in which we were walking, she leading me by the hand through a forest. She was naked and walked tall and barefoot through the trees and all around us I could see women in long robes with their faces covered. With her long limbs she walked over branches and twigs and earth without breaking stride and beneath her feet I cold hear the snapping of branches. We neared a small clearing by a shore and I could see the lake (it was a lake! the things we know in dreams!) was frozen and when we reached the shore I felt her grip loosen on my hand and naked she dove through the sheet of snow-blown ice and disappeared beneath the surface, never turning once to face me.

I woke in the centre of the bed, with the sunlight coming softly through the tall floor-to-ceiling white curtains puddled on the floor. The blanket was white and with the clicking of the white radiator I felt as though I were the projector of this dream, spinning with film off the reel. I was alone, and naked among the matted white screens where the dream had occurred.

After my meeting Hissel by the lilac trees outside of the church, he went silent for two weeks. I took long walks around the city, passing the cafés or benches where we met but there was nothing. My arm was healing, but that didn't mean I had fully quit the gear. I was losing weight, and the walks were getting harder. In a futile move of self-atonement for the self-abuse, or perhaps as a way just to facilitate it, I picked up a cheap bicycle at a nearby market and used it to ride through the streets at night feeling the snow against my face as it lightly fell while I looked for any sign of Hissel. When I finally did see him, he was sitting across from me on a train, his head rocking from side to side as the train bent its way into the city.

15

Berlin. December 29

I don't know how long he'd been across from me on the train or
how long he had been on the same train just watching me but I
suppose it didn't matter. He motioned for me to get off the train
and after I did so, we walked mostly in silence to a café in Prenz-
lauerberg, a once-punk neighbourhood slowly gentrified after
the wall came down, overtaken by boutiques, ice cream parlours
and expensive furniture shops. He was perfectly out of place. But
he had cleaned up, and blended in well in the neighbourhood.
When we'd meet in Treptow or Wedding and he dressed in his
sweatpants, boots, and jean jacket, he fit in just fine, looking like
any number of low-income townies or artists that made Berlin
their home. But here he fit right in. He had a button-down shirt
I could see beneath the buttoned denim jacket he wore under a
blazer. Pressed slacks he'd lifted from God only knows where.
The same boots, only polished. He almost looked normal with
the squared-off shoulders of the blazer over his skinny frame. It
was hard to believe he'd been a soldier. Impossible even. But I'd
seen the drugs do this to men. Hollow them. They'd half eaten
me. He wore a wool cap over a pair of auburn-framed sunglasses
with dark lenses. His beard had been cut slightly and rested on
the thick crimson scarf tied neatly around his neck. Black gloves
Always the black leather gloves. Never once did I see his hands.

We followed the scent of perfume of a young woman who rode
her bicycle past us. The kind of scent you'd follow over a cliff if you
weren't careful. The bell on her bicycle rang lightly as the wheels
shook over the cobblestone street, and when men turned their
heads to see her, they didn't turn away. We arrived at a small Russian

restaurant and took a table outside. Hissel went inside to use the washroom and when he came out I couldn't take my eyes off him. He was standing there with the sun at his back and I squinted to make out his figure. Those narrow shoulders and waist, the slightly hunched back, with his hands by his side. He stood there for a moment and I watched him take a few breaths as he stared at me. He came and sat down beside me. When the waiter came he ordered a water. He was pleasant, like the sun had got into him. We didn't say much. Just sat facing south, letting the late afternoon sun hit our faces. I ordered a coffee and when it came, I gave him the details for the third and final name, a bonus job but just for him, and a small cash advance. The location. The flat number. The date. The time. And an unusual request about the method.

The details smarted him. "I'd like to know why." He was staring straight ahead. He didn't make eye contact with me once while we spoke about that job.

"Don't worry about it."

"Just strange is all. Seems you know this guy more than others know most. Got him right down to the placement of his boots."

"Maybe I'm not such a novice." I hadn't spoken once of the final target on my list. But Hissel wasn't stupid either. A loose cannon, for sure, if that's what he even was. "Go to the address in this envelope. You can open it now if you want. The key is inside. The rest will be there waiting for you there. Stay for a coffee after if you want."

"I won't stay."

"Suit yourself," I said. "If there aren't two boots by the door and a single coat on a hook you can turn around no questions asked."

"And you're sure he'll be in the bath at that time."

"Yes."

"Sounds like a trap."

"I promise it's not a trap." Hissel was silent for a moment. "I take one of your cigarettes now."

I opened the box and he reached in with his gloved hand and took one. I leaned towards him and lit it for him with my lighter, holding the flame to his face as he inhaled. I tried to look into his eyes but could only see myself and the flame in the reflection of his sunglasses. He leaned back, and faced away from me, taking a few more drags.

"One thing," he said. "Where did you go after Japan?"

"Back to Montreal."

"Why?"

"Different reasons. To regroup. I thought maybe there were answers there but there weren't. It wasn't long before I could find assignments. Over time, my options grew. But in the end, I took the most remote job they had."

"Did you have a death wish or something?"

"I don't know. No. I wasn't afraid to die. I was indifferent. I wanted distraction. Afghanistan seemed the right call."

"So you never knew you would find her there?"

"No."

"But you did."

"I found a fragment of her there. First, I found her in a box. In an old photo. The two of us by a campfire. One of those photos you find in a box inside a box. I wasn't looking for her. I was unpacking a blanket soon after I moved back to Montreal — more like a large sheet we would spread on the grass in the park there."

"What did you do alone in Montreal?"

"It was summer. I moved my work to the park. Wrote my stories in a notebook. Made up quotes. Typed them at the library and filed them and then would sit in the park at night and drink or smoke up on Mount Royal."

"Sounds like important place."

"It was. I'd once been a king and she a queen there."

"Because you were popular?"

"No. Because we were alone and no one knew us and nothing else mattered but us."

"Tell me about the first time you were with her."

"Don't be a pervert, Hissel."

He smiled and clicked his dentures.

"Show me her through your eyes. We'll never see each other again so why does it matter to you?"

And so I told Hissel. I spoke staring straight ahead as he bowed
his head to listen to me, about what it was like to be inside of
her. About how when we were eighteen she was back from
theatre school in her first year for Thanksgiving but had come
home unannounced to find her parents were away and called
me up to meet in a park where we sat on a picnic table outside
the tennis courts in the park close to midnight drinking cheap
wine and how she'd brought a corkscrew and two small glasses
and she kept her head down when a pair of men were exiting
the tennis courts to keep from seeing one of them, a man in a
blue track jacket, who'd passed us without seeing her and how
this made her feel forgettable again because once when they'd
dated he'd ended things because she wasn't quite pretty enough.
I told Hissel about how it had been a humid night for October
and the police left us alone as they drove along the sidewalk and
she sat hidden inside her fur-lined camouflage parka sipping on
that cheap wine while her bangs hung just above her eyes and
how together we talked about how neither of us knew where we
really were, that we were just islands upon the island, an archipelago of sadness among the junkies and joggers who passed
us under the orange glow archways of flung cigarette butts and
how I could barely see her face as she sat silhouetted in front of
the floodlights of the tennis courts in her white Slazenger socks
pulled high above her boots and how when we stood up to part
ways, a little chilly and a little drunk I told her how wrong he was,
how wrong the man in the blue track jacket was, and how when
she gave me a hug to say goodbye it was clear how much better it
felt just to stay there with our bodies pressed together and how
when we finished the bottle of that cheap wine at her parents'
empty house she made me make a million promises and I swore
I'd keep every one of them starting with the first one I made that
Thursday night and that I when I went back to my apartment it
was a Monday in the same clothes and by January we took what
savings we had and booked the cheapest flight we could find to

the farthest place from anywhere, landing in Ecuador, where we took any shit jobs we could find, and that soon we were running a rental home owned by a retired American woman who let us stay for free if we ran the place but who was really giving us the keys to our own small world on the long wide beach of Santa Marianita where the waves hammered the shore day and night, where going to town meant hitching rides in the back of pickup-truck-taxis into the main city of Manta to load up on groceries. I told him that for a short time the Pacific Ocean was all ours, that we stayed there for months and then moved farther down the coast, found a surf town and rented the top floor of a pension for ten dollars a night and which was a short walk to the beach and in the daytime we would swim between the surfers and in the evenings we would nap and then eat cheap dinners of plantains, rice, and lentil stew at the open restaurants and afterwards we'd make a small fire on the beach and sit there beneath the stars, sometimes sleeping there until the last embers burned out, waking up not far from where the wild horses would lie on the sand not far from us while the morning waves lapped quietly on the shore. I told him that I had no idea how long we stayed there, that it was weeks or maybe months, until the winds changed and the surfers left and the wind chilled and the skies were more grey than blue, a sign that summer was coming in the north and that we searched for a cheap flight to Europe and left from the capital after a ten-hour bus ride through the Andes mountains where Quechua women in colourful shawls and bowler hats boarded at every stop selling grilled pork and mote in small brown paper bags before the next thing we knew we were somehow a continent and an ocean away from the mountains and volcanoes of Quito on an all-night train from Madrid to Marseille where we stripped in our cabin and slept the entire way. She had a friend there and once in Marseille we peeled off our clothes once again this time to swim between the boats of a harbour close to where her friend lived and later there, in the fog of exhaustion we made our way across the rocky coastlines of the Mediterranean, inching our way to the south of Italy where we ferried to Greece and then rested again, this time in a tent on the beach I could never find again on an island I could never name again before we finally took a flight to Tel Aviv and I told Hissel that it was this, that it was all of this, the sum total of those fields and faces we passed in the miles traversed across two and a half continents, that it was the millions of litres of salt water that buoyed us in the waves of the Pacific Ocean under full moons to feed a promise made one night in an empty house in Montreal, that it was all of these together which was what it was like to be inside of her.

We stayed with friends of hers in Tel Aviv, friends in a small dance company there who took us in and fed us and made us beds on their living room floors, friends of hers who took us to their favourite clubs and how on the dance floors, dripping with youth, we thought we had the answer, how asleep on those secluded beaches we thought we had the answer, how in bed, with our bodies connected we thought we had the answer. But we never never did. Because in Tel Aviv things were about to change forever and from that moment on there would not be answers only darkness.

"The only thing that gets clearer when you get older," I said. "You spend half your life thinking you have life figured out only to realize that all you're really doing is collecting pieces of an answer you'll never know the question to."

"The price of admission."

"To what?"

"Life."

"The brutality is that the final piece of that puzzle isn't even death."

"What is it then?" he asked.

"It's accepting that you'll never have answers. That you're entitled to nothing. That you'll always only be in the dark."

"Or maybe that's the beauty."

"What's fucking beautiful about the dark?" I said.

My eyes were closed but I could feel him there. So I kept on.

"I used to be able to remember her, more of her. But every year I lose more and more of her."

"Try," Hissel said.

"She's on a dock on Lake Memphremagog. It was summer. The sun was coming off the water with blinding light. She was statuesque on those waters and with the glare of the sun you could barely make out that she was standing on a dock at all. She was just there. On the surface of the water, staring out. Terry cloth shorts and some old undersized vintage T-shirt. I dipped my foot into the water and though it was July the lake was cold but the next thing I remember she was pulling the T-shirt over her head and then rolling her shorts down her legs as long as the goddamn pine trees on the horizon. For a moment, naked on the dock, it was just her standing on what seemed like the surface of the water staring straight into the sun, before her knees bent slightly and her arms were above her head as she dove forward. I remember her long back and her long legs bare beneath the surface of the lake, her incredibly long strokes beneath the water as she slowly vanished into the glare coming off the water, and the dock swaying gently with the waves she'd left in her wake."

"What else?"

"She is standing in a group at a party. I don't even know whose party it is but we're in a Montreal apartment and it's New Year's Eve. She's in a black wool turtleneck dress talking to a group of people and her eyes catch mine."

"What do you remember next?"

"What do you care?"

"I want everything," he said.

"We're on a fire escape and it's cold and we're smoking cigarettes or maybe a joint."

"And then?"

"We're by the fire in my courtyard — it's fall and she's going to leave again. There's a bag of beers by her side which she's brought. Like some kind of half-date but there's a party in one of the apartments in the courtyard and I remember this because I had to translate another neighbour yelling at the people at the party. I can't remember who was French and who was English but one was having fun and the other was trying to sleep and in the middle of it all were the two of us, in the courtyard, sitting beside the fire pit filled with the glowing embers of barbeque coals. It was illegal to make a fire but there was no law against filling it with coals and I remember carrying the bag over my shoulder up St. Laurent Boulevard from the all-night supermarket earlier that evening. But after a while her bag of beer was empty and her cough was getting louder so we moved inside into my room and listened to music in the dark. It was the last time I was young. Nothing was the same after that. For her too."

"What do you remember next?"

"Just the music — and then how what started as two bodies chilled from the night outside became two beneath the blankets with the moonlight coating her skin in silver light in the shadows of that basement apartment."

"And then?"

"That's it."

"That's not it. There's more."

"Her elbows in the air as she tied her hair back before lowering herself on top of me. The force of those elbows on my clavicles as she dug her face into my neck and her knees into my hips. The sound of her breath like wind through a highway tunnel. The curve of her back in the morning as she dressed, the trench of her spine as her back arched while sliding into a dress before leaving to catch a plane. I remember hating that this was the way it would always be with us. That she was always leaving and I was always left wondering if this was the last time I would ever see her. It was the same feeling I had as we lay in bed in a Brooklyn apartment months later when all we had was three days together and I drove across sidewalks to get to her when the snow was so high it was killing people but it was worth it just to feel her tongue she drove deep into my mouth when we kissed because for her there was only one way to kiss a lover. That's it. That's all you're fucking getting. Hold him below the water. He's weak. And sick."

"What if he fights."

"He won't fight."

"I'm not as strong as I used to be."

"Then you can shoot him. But better that he drowns. That the water fills his lungs. He'll thrash but not for long. It's normal. The body's natural response."

"You see? To fight."

"No. To lessen the trauma. The limbs thrash to exhaust the body of oxygen. It makes death come faster."

"Funny that."

"What?"

"The body. Always trying to protect the thing inside. How it makes a man pass out when the pain gets too much. Trauma gets suppressed. Accidents get erased from memory. Only come back when soul is ready for it. Or maybe it's other way around, and the soul decides."

"And when the good memories get lost?" I asked. "What is that?"

"I don't know. Old age I guess. Maybe forgetting is the soul's way of not letting someone spend too much time in the past."

"So then what? We should be grateful when we forget people?"

"I don't know. Maybe all this is Hell and life is just a competition to suffer less than the next man."

I got up to leave. I left the bag at Hissel's feet and said goodbye without looking at him.

16

Berlin. December 29. 11:00pm

I walked until my legs burned, along Bernauer Strasse, past the tall iron skeletal remains of the Berlin Wall. It was night-time and the weather was a mix of rain and snow. I thought my knees would dislocate if I took another step. I crouched on the street to force some blood into the joints and rest my back. Then made the final haul to a nearby bar where my world was about to come to pieces.

The TV was on low and I ordered a beer and finished half of it at once. Outside: sleet, and shit. I waited for what felt like forever until my hookup arrived. Inside the bathroom where we made the exchange the temperature was colder than it was inside the bar, so much so that, when I pissed after making the exchange, my hands felt warm from the steam rising from the urinal. My urine was pink with blood but it was no matter now. In a moment I would return to my barstool and my world would come brutally apart.

I went back to the barstool and caught a story on the silent television behind the bar. My German was shit but I knew enough to catch the phrases of the captions and figure out what was going on and when I did I felt my heart stop and my body turn cold. The story was of the remains of a German soldier discovered by the bank of the Amu River with three bullets in his back. There was an enlarged photo of the man, a stock military photo with Hissel's name, rank, and division attached to it. The story was too much of a coincidence for this not to be my Hissel but the man in the photograph on TV was not the Hissel I'd met on the bridge, it was not the Hissel I'd spent the last months with. The Hissel on

TV was dead, with three bullets in his back and now it was clear
I was being conned out of my money by a sack-of-shit junkie vet
with a story he'd probably picked up on tour. I had let my guard
down, way way down, and I was furious. If I ever saw Hissel again
I would kill him and I let the hate grow inside me and fester and
I asked the bartender to change the channel and pour me more
drinks. I sat on that miserable barstool trying to backpedal to see
where I'd gone wrong. I was a goddamn fool and it was plain as
miserable day that this man was a soldier who had undoubtedly
heard of the missing soldier and prisoner, a story he'd carried
back and sold to me like a second-hand car in exchange for almost
everything I had. I knew nothing and wanted everything and he
knew that and capitalized on it. I'd been a fool to ask him so soon
about the work I was asking him about. But I'd been desperate. I
don't know how long I'd been nosing around Berlin looking for
a clue or a face for the names I'd been given. I was already a dead
man. A dead man tricked by the devil chasing the names handed
to him by a ghost. I turned my face to the mirror behind the bar
and it was a stranger looking back at me. I'd come to Berlin delu-
sional, no different than the junkies howling barefoot on the tram
tracks, only instead of howling at invisible monsters I'd arrived
with a monster of a fantasy that I would somehow be God's dark
agent of vengeance and with humiliating clarity I was able to see
myself as others saw me, and as Hissel no doubt saw me. I'd un-
loaded money to my own personal howler who could see early on
I was one of his own.

I drank until they threw me out and when I got back to the flat, I
was profusely ill. As I lay with my face on the cold floor, I made
no effort to move when I felt my stomach lurch and empty on
the floor next to my face. I came to peace with Hissel before I
finally passed out. There was no other way. The money I'd paid
him was a tax for the delusion I would no longer be living out. I
had enough to make sure the next days would be my last.

17.

That night, I climbed the black iron stairs in the alley. I rolled up my sleeve and unwrapped the bandage, dropping it from the top of the stairs in the alley. I watched as it slowly landed among the snow and garbage in the alley below. I held the needle between my thumb and forefinger and counted the ninety-nine steps, but went deeper into the skin each time. When I reached the top of my forearm, blood was running down my arm and dripping from my fingertips. I extended my thumb but held it there on the plunger. Across the alley two dancers were rehearsing in a loft. I could hear the arpeggiated minor chords on an acoustic guitar as the two bodies intertwined, moving as one and then away from each other. Their tights were beige, and they appeared nude as the flickering fluorescent lights hanging from the cement ceiling above them accentuated the muscles on their slender bodies. I watched them through the thin dirty panes between the red brick exterior. He was thin, but with a wide muscular back, a thin sculpted face and boyish wavy hair. She had muscular legs and a disproportionately thin torso typical of dancers. Her hair was pulled back into a tight bun which made her age ambiguous. She could have been fourteen, or forty, though the way she moved suggested she was the latter, as she moved like a woman with history rather than as a girl counting steps. The studio was above a launderette and as they danced on the second floor I could see a woman folding laundry alone below. I pulled the hood over my head and rested my head on the iron railing of the fire escape and let my eyes wander high above the launderette and the studio into the flickering grid of lights from the high rises of the next block. There were thousands of people in those buildings, their presence signalled by the lights from their apartments, yet I could see no one and so I turned my eyes back to the dancers, my thumb still on the plunger and the blood still trailing down my arm. I would wake in the morning. I would walk back to the flat, get cleaned up, try to keep a breakfast down. Then I would score a final time.

18

Berlin. December 31st. 11:48pm

I'm woken by the chilling of the water in the bath. This bathroom. These tiles. A photo in a cracked frame on a wall. Black and white. It could have been taken fifty years ago, a hundred even, summer, spring. But I remember the day the photo was taken, standing in second-hand clothes and a wool hat, asking some local to take my photo.

I reach for the taps and then down more wine by the tub. The porcelain is cold against the back. I refill the tub and sit shivering as the water goes down the drain. I stare at the candle straight ahead and remember when once it was a fire and the warmth of your face against mine and I was close enough to map the flecks of your eyes. When we were face to face in the sleeping bag on the side of the highway in the holy land, the chill of the wind against our skin in the cold Negev desert where there was only one way to stay warm and I was your blonde hair and tightly wound curls and night turned everything black and later when you were asleep after you told me to sleep inside you I made sure the fire kept going to keep us warm until daybreak when we had to pack up the car and be back on the road.

19

Tel Aviv. 2001

When we made it to the Dead Sea we covered our bodies in the mud from head to toe and stank like sulphur and later that night as we showered together after the long drive back to Tel Aviv I ran my fingers through her hair and it felt like silk. I'd never felt anything that soft and she said it was from the mud. Later that night we went walking on the beach and I said something about how soft the sand was and we stood there moving our toes in the sand and digging our feet in as deep as we could with every step. We sat down, cupping that powder-soft sand and letting it run between our fingers while we listened to the waves hit the shore until the sky began to break. We slept all day, showered again and then later went dancing at a gay nightclub she'd been told was great. It was, and after a short wait in line we went inside where there was a mixed and friendly crowd. She disappeared into the bathroom with a man and when she came back she handed me a little white pill with a small white dove on it and after an hour or so I felt light as air and it was the last time I would ever feel a lightness that pure and unburdened, no matter how many times I tried to find it again. We went back to her friends' flat in the morning, friends who'd agreed to let us stay there and we smoked joints on their rooftops to come down as Apache helicopters flew overhead. She sold her friends on the nightclub and we made plans to meet them there later the following night. But when they got there, and while she and I sat on the beach listening to the waves with that soft sand beneath our bodies, an explosion tore through the nightclub killing every single one of them.

From the beach we could hear the explosion and the lights of the sirens could be seen above the low buildings and in her eyes I could see the earth chasm, exposing a precipice into which she'd fall and never climb out. That morning I bought two tickets to Eilat on the coast and packed our bags and stuffed a few bottles of cheap vodka from a shop nearby and when we arrived in Eilat, I put us on a bus that crossed us into Sinai. I found us a ride and we drove slowly through the desert in the back of a pickup truck and above us the stars just hung there. I tried to hold her and I got her elbows and soon she was sitting up in the cab of the truck just staring back at the road which unrolled in front of us and for the rest of the night we just drove further and further from where we'd started, drawing closer into the darkness of what was to come. When we were around halfway between Eilat and Sharm El Sheik, I befriended a Sudanese man who led me down a long, secluded beach to an empty restaurant where I traded the vodka with a restaurant manager for marijuana. He got the marijuana from the local Bedouin and could sell the vodka I was giving him to the tourists. We were a short drive to Mount Sinai where religious pilgrims assembled but we never left the village. I suggested we take a taxi there, just to see it, but she wanted nothing to do with it. So we sat in the cafés, and she played backgammon like a robot and when it got hot or the throngs of kids became too much she walked without announcement into the sea among the snakes, the eels and the lionfish, silent killers beneath the surface of the sea, from whom later she'd take her cue. The current was strong and I sliced my feet on the coral trying to reach her.

She barely said a word those following weeks. We took a long bus to Cairo and at the airport there was a mix-up at the gate. The flight was overbooked and at the last minute she gave away my seat while I was in the washroom washing off the sweat and the dirt from my face. She handed me my new ticket and before I knew what was going on she was boarding and waved once and never turned back. I looked for her at the airport when I arrived home from the flight the next day, but she wasn't there and I had no number to reach her at. My emails went unanswered and after that summer I found out she'd dropped out of theatre school, changed her major in university, traded her dance shoes and theatre masks for lab coats and by winter she was on an exchange in Paris. We wouldn't meet again for seven years, when she turned up in Montreal, under an umbrella outside a friend's place I was housesitting.

20.

Berlin. December 31ˢᵗ, 11:57pm

Syringa. What role would you be playing on a theatre stage right now? What mask would you be wearing? Would you have finished theatre school like you'd wanted to and not become enchanted by politics at university? Would you still be a dancer? Would you be the wolf that climbed on top of me in the back seat of a station wagon while our friends sat in the front seat driving? When bursting with youth in the back seat somewhere on a desert highway in the Promised Land was beautiful and not to be questioned.

Part of you died in that disco with your friends. When a bomb tore the place to pieces and they could never bury all of them. After you graduated you went straight into grad school overseas and the last I heard after that you were writing the Foreign Service exam.

The candle flickers. Burns out. I see the door. How it moves in the light. And there's the feeling that this room is not a room but a prison. That this is Hell. That everything is a lie. That this candle is a lie. That this water is a lie. Every face. Every eyelash. A lie. Every single bead of sweat. A lie. That you get on a train. A lie. That you leave in a black SUV in New York. A lie. That you disappear behind the red velvet curtain of a Tel Aviv disco. A lie. That the sun goes down. A lie.

When I flew back from Egypt, alone, I remember sitting in the corner of the waiting room of the airport before take-off. I wore a baseball cap which I pulled over my eyes and I let the tears roll down my face. I knew you'd be gone when the plane landed. I sat there in that airplane seat, my heart volcanic as the plane shook inside the clouds as the plane descended, trying to calculate the sum of a life which had torn me first from a drowning mother in a car sinking in the icy waters of Lake Ontario, with an improbable love which at its peak felt like having my arms torn off my body when you left, and somehow the answer was nothing.

The day I arrived in Berlin I found a café, a massive space with old furniture, and took a seat in the corner, but it slowly filled and as it did the music which came over the tinny speakers over my head felt as though they'd been plucked from that Tel Aviv flat before everything went south. Song after song. It was haunting and there I was again, volcanic again, with my hat pulled low over my eyes with songs which I thought were buried on a mixed tape in a land-fill squeezing tear after tear from my eyes, unable to control myself, to control the world around me, to control a history which had radicalized you the day a bomb tore through a disco and your papier mâché masks of ancient Greek dramas became the masks you then wore in a sweltering theatre of biblical violence.

But then there is light. The flickering candle and the memory of you dancing — oh the memory of you dancing — when I lay on the floor in the corner of the room where cushions were enough and you were a giant hovering above me, bathed in song, with your long limbs moving in concert with the universe and how I sailed through the days away from you with nothing but the memory of you dancing.

21

Berlin. December 31st. 11:59pm

When a man drowns there is no fighting the panic created by apnea. His body wants to panic because it knows death is better than the trauma. Exhaust the body of oxygen so it slips into unconsciousness. Levels of carbon dioxide increase, leading to a stronger breathing reflex, until holding the breath is no longer possible and that final fateful gasp for impossible air is taken and the lungs fill with water. Water enters the lungs, restricting the absorption of oxygen and asphyxia occurs, followed by cerebral hypoxia and myocardial infarction. The next event to occur if the victim is conscious when they start drowning is laryngospasm. The larynx constricts and seals the air tube.

My mother felt all of these things. And she remained still. Keeping me there in her arms. While my father was clawing at a sheet of ice above him.

At this point, prior to the severe biochemical disruptions and inevitable cardiac arrest, there is a period where the victim is said to experience a state of peace. A state of bliss. Did my mother feel this? As she held her child. As she breathed warm air into its lungs until her own lungs were empty. I remember now. A song. A song in the front seat while sitting on my mother's lap. Coming through the tinny speakers before it cut out.

Severe biochemical disruptions precede silent cardiac arrest, but the drug is stronger than the fight. And so peace. An orange light in the hallway illuminating the corners of a picture frame as the wall flickers blue with the lights of a police car passing the building outside.

The candle flickers from beneath the water, and lashing memory against memory where our feet touch on a bus as we sleep in double seats across the aisle. When you undress by the sea. When you fly down a hill on a bicycle. Or smile from a beach in Ecuador. When I came back from Afghanistan I got clean in Montreal and I got messy again. I tried running to the country but I haunted myself in those woods. So I came back to the city and went to war with myself and when the war seemed lost I'd caught wind of the New Year's summit in Berlin and I chose it as the city of a multitude of deaths.

And so I gave in. I watched that candle flicker.

I watched those memories collide and shatter before my eyes as my heart slowed.

A kiss outside your father's house. The scent of lilacs exploding to life in early summer.

Traffic outside the window now and droplets of water leave the tile. Footsteps down the hall. Every face. The crackle of wood by the roadside. Two bodies in a sleeping bag. Your body, napping in a hammock after swimming in the sea.

Every face.

Every eyelash.

Every single bead of sweat.

When you were there. With me. When there was meat on the bone. Tendons firing. Fat on the hips, and your knees digging tighter into my ribcage as the muscles in your back tightened and your forearms curled tighter around my neck. I could have died there in your grip and you'd have never known. The blood could have seeped between your fingers and you'd have never known. Not while in your heart the sirens wailed, and tanks snapped through barbed wire and the landmines detonated in the cosmic space between the atoms in your body, not as the windows shattered in your bloodstream and the petrol in the cars we played with as children caught fateful flame and the dishes fell from the cupboards of the books we were read as children, not while the screams of children in our old class photos drowned out the sound of machine gun fire and church bells and holy choirs and fire trucks all swirling in your throat with the palm trees and camels and sand, life vests, and orchids and flotillas and silk when out from your mouth came fleets of vessels and flies, Korans and Rabbinic verses, sacred beads and spices and wooden heeled shoes, steaming metal pots and overboiled herbs, ornaments, and falcons flapping their wings as the fireworks tore holes in the walls and exploded over this city, illuminating everything, the orb of perspiration along your jawline and the ice cold fact that we would never meet again.

Until Hissel.

Hissel.

Those eyes through the water. My half ghost half wreckage friend, who puts his hand on my shoulders and never takes them off for a second. Not while the earth opens beneath our feet. Not while the bath deepens and the water rises over my face. Not with that look in his eyes that says I hadn't found him but he

had found me and needed me as much as I needed him and that
sometimes, just sometimes, the stars align. Hissel, with eyes that
say I have no reason to be sorry or nothing to fear. He puts his
thin fingers on my cheeks, on my lips, He leans forward with his
feet in the tub then pulls my legs together and straddles me. He
leans forward and the water sloshes as he comes closer to my
face and his breath is like the warmth from a fire. I feel his hands
on my face and his bony elbows dig into my shoulders and all
his weight is on me now and I feel the water enter my ears but
nothing else and the only sound is the final contractions of my
heart and under the water I feel his wet beard on my face as he
moves his skinny arms under my head and his face draws near
with that heavy wet beard until his salty lips are on mine and
then there's nothing but a surge of warm air from his lungs inside
my mouth our two hearts charged back to life for the final surge
towards death that's thunder in my ears with lips sinking below
the surface as my lungs empty and I feel those slender arms below my neck as he brings my face above the water again and in
his eyes I see the faces of the two men I tried desperately to find
but couldn't but whom he had found and he whispers in my ears
the three sentences that hurt more than death and he smiles with
mouth pulled wide and wet with tears connecting our two faces
with the clarity of a cold still lake and the words I love you I love
you I love you but there is no going back, that there is never going back, there is only going forward and that by morning we'd
both be free, when the swell of sirens takes over everything as
the echo of an explosion as far away as Unter den Linden fills the
bathroom and then his warm tongue is in my mouth as our faces
sink again beneath the water and it's a tongue I swear I've tasted
a thousand times before.

In the photo of Hissel on television he stood beneath a canopy
of purple Lilacs. In time, authorities would be led to that small
cottage registered in his family name, where I lost him the day I'd

tailed him and what a treat they would find there. They would look past the Christmas lights and toy car parts and think nothing of the boxes of nails until the sum of the rest of the parts inside the cottage finally added up. Junked cell phones and boxes of batteries, coils of scavenged electrical wire and circuit boards. The buckets of aluminium foil and bags of rice flour. Empty tubs of chemicals, and steel wool. The small fireplace with the Duraflame logs stacked next to it, coffee grinders, and shards of metal shavings would show that whatever went on in here was way off the radar of German hobby gardening. They'd find a small chair at a table with a mirror and battery-run light with makeup brushes and bottles of liquid silicone, adhesives, foam latex and rolls of crepe wool next to barber's sheers, an iron, curing agents and gelatine solutions. Small bottles overturned and painkillers in unmarked bottles. Whoever was using this place would enter with one face and leave with another, sleeping here and keeping some sort of ultra-downsized life going while they planned for this night. With each explosion drowning out the smaller explosions of fireworks colouring the sky above the city, I felt arms around my body tighten and the water leave my lungs.

Hissel.

Hissel.

Whisper your name and it sounds like a kiss.

When did I really meet you for the first time? In the showers of the YMCA as a four-year-old? Was that you, immense in the steam, your head tilted back, as my mother dressed nearby?

Was that you when summer's end was a galaxy away and it was millennia before your parents packed the car and I was chasing your station wagon on my small bicycle as you waved goodbye from the wide back window? You, that summer, when we slept on the beach under countless Ontario stars when summer never ended and no one ever died and love was not punishable by death?

You, in terry cloth shorts and a ten-speed bike with red-rimmed glasses and socks pulled high?

Was that you, with the wolf on your cut-off T-shirt, with shoulders glowing with perspiration, making the windows rattle and fog as music pounded all around us in the discos before they ever caught sacrilegious fire?

Was that you, the last woman on the dance floor in a fire-engine red dress sliding a quarter in the jukebox and saying don't leave me alone on the dance floor tonight?

You! playing bocce in the back alley of the rainbow district after dark drinking wine from the bottle and arguing the calls with long black wavy hair over your face and a cigarette dangling from your wine-stained lips as jazz records rang out from the balcony above us.

Was that you with the auburn freckles and cherrywood dress and the orchestral sounds of the café in the morning and the low metallic drone of a dishwasher behind you?

You! at the party when our eyes met momentarily as you told a story, waving your hands in the air with those eyes like bursting nebulae.

You! The place where there is no such thing as time. Locked in a place that moves further from me every day.

I was with you every minute of the day when you were gone. In your skin, in the nape of your neck, in the pocket of your over-sized coat, next to the lighter you flicked while coconut soup simmered on the stove with a pile of dishes in the sink behind you and ashes piled in the empty wine bottle, I was there, in the towel you wore around your neck after dance class.

It was you in that flat, three days in Montreal that summer lying in our underwear listening to soul records on the CBC. You, your long limbs, your black bra as we sat by the fan to cool our sticky skin. You, when there were no words only food. Your cinnamon and vanilla rice milk skin. Your coconut eyes. Warm honeydew tongue.

You! when the snowflakes were falling around us. The alcohol keeping us warm. Your arms around me and my lips millimetres from your face. In a week you'd be gone. You'd travel over the Atlantic to study and I wouldn't see you again until the day I pedalled past you as you lay on the bank of a lake where I wouldn't even know it was you.

I searched the world and three times you were there, right under my nose before I found you again on the platform of a Kyoto train station. Once on your back with your gold skin facing the sun on the bank of the Spree. How did I not recognize you? Once behind oversized sunglasses as you left on the back of a scooter in Nice. How did I not recognize that neck in time?

It was also you. Dancing alone in a subway that night.

And you, flying down a hill on a rainy afternoon in skin-tight jeans. One hand on the handlebars, the other on the long end of a headscarf arched over your head to guard you from the rain.

You. Every face and every eyelash. You in every single bead of sweat. You, in a tan raincoat getting on a train. You, disappearing behind the red velvet curtain of a Tel Aviv disco. You, standing topless, waist high in the sea with the giant brim of that hat covering your face You! you! you! whenever the sun went down. Whenever the sun came up.

And then, you in the silence. You and the crunching of pebbles under the wheels of a cab on the wet street. You and the damp cloth along the inside of a wine glass. You when there were no voices of women. You where there was no muffled chatter of men. You and the clatter of saucers. You and the old tinny rhythm and blues on a café stereo. You, the rushing of the water and your silhouette before the fountain, backlit by the floodlight before our slow walk to watch the tango dancers on the bank where boats pass by the museum. You, the long drapes. You, the large room. You, the birds chirping at daybreak. You when there were no typewriter keys hammering the ribbon. You, no bed, no bodies pressed together in the night. You you you and the click click click on the cobblestone street. You, a warm breath and chatter by the dock. You, peeling off your clothes to dive naked in the waters of Lac Memphremagog saying on the count of three let's jump in together and I can still taste your breath if I close my eyes. I can still see those emerald eyes, and the blood in your hair, and your voice like a cello.

You stopped for nothing.

Not for the kids who called you a monster when all you wanted were friends or their parents who told you to speak white when all you spoke was French.

Not for the doctor who pulled down your pants when you were four and put his finger inside you and never took it out.

Not for the university counsellor tossing testers of Paxil at you when all you needed was to talk.

Not for your husband who shook you until your hair turned white.

Not for the men who whipped you with the cables after they dragged you away from me.

Not for my heart that beat to the point of explosion whenever I was around you.

You stopped for none of that.

You never screamed once for them when they tied you to the chair in the prison and not once did you unclench your fist. And ten thousand years from now when your body is unearthed by the bank of a the river where flowers grow wild and impossibly thick, your knuckles will still be curled and beneath the fractured ribcage of dirt-dry skeleton will they see with great mystery how a beating heart still soaks the soil with blood and the petals of the poppies in the fields trail crimson ink on the fingertips of those who hold them before they fall back down to earth and shake the ground the beneath their feet.

You will never not be a part of me, Syringa.

I searched endlessly for you but you were always all around me. In the wooden-heeled boots that go click click click. Mitochondrial, you were a part of me.

but the last sound I hear is the sloshing of those boots in the water and then that voice whispering "Shhhhhhh … Listen" as I hear the bomb as it goes off and tears apart the hotel room where the men who traded love for power were tied with cables to a chair.

"Shhhhh"

Taste burnt enamel as it crackles on the teeth, hear the wobble of the organs, shuffled painfully beneath the ribs which splinter beneath the burning flesh.

"Shhhhh"

Slow nut and bolt and glass in the air as cables melt into the flesh amid the smell of burning hair.

"Shhhhh"

Hear the rubble coat the avenue and the sprinkle of glass a thousand feet away.

"Shhhhh"

While there's still enough life to feel the burning liquification of the eyes.

22

New Year's Day.

I wake up cold and wet, naked beneath a blanket on the bath-room floor. I pull myself up from the floor and find clothes in the other room and dress. I slide my boots on without socks and keep the blanket around my shoulders as I walk outside. I take in the sight of the city. Everywhere the garbage and the wreckage. Everywhere the stink of sulphur and piss among the shattered beer bottles and Champagne bottles on their side. Outside, fire-works casings everywhere. Barely a soul in sight. Church bells ring out from a far-off church tower. Across Berlin, all that is left of last night's parties is the clanging of bottles on the street or the crunch of broken glass in the cracks of stony sidewalks. I pass a café with a television on and can make out the balconies on the screen in tatters, hanging like loose teeth, and bicycles twisted on the fence poles before the smouldering remains of a burned-out floor of a building. I pull the blanket tighter around my shoulders. Skyline smoking, my body shivers as light cascades where the clouds open up. I feel the snow beneath my boots and can hear sirens blocks away before spotting a figure behind me in the reflection of the window.

When they discovered the remains of the two men at the em-bassy party tied to the chair with cords, they suspected the killer wouldn't be far away. And they weren't wrong, just unable to pull a face from the crowd, as the rubble was swept away, right there, on the same street, as the killer stood there, under their noses and under the lilac trees, with long hair pulled loosely back in a ponytail, and with the warm daytime sun against her tender neck, unlocking the rickety bicycle, feeling the gravel crumble beneath the tires beneath the trees across from Brandenberg Gate, disappearing in the shadows of the old hunting fields of Tiergarten, past the Victory statue, with her golden wings spread high over the city as the killer's heart beat beneath the breast-bone, with legs growing warmer with each forceful push upon the pedals, as I stand on the street somehow reborn, muttering the same words, over and over:

Syringa.

Syringa.

I will never forget you.

I will never forget you.

Acknowledgements

The author would like to express his gratitude to Guernica publisher, Michael Mirolla, and editor Julie Roorda, as well as Rafael Chimicatti for the cover design. To the Canada Council for their support, and to Noah Richler for early guidance on the manuscript. Most importantly, he would like to thank his family for enduring with him, the often arduous process of novel writing.

About the Author

IAN ORTI is the author of short novels and shorter stories. His work has been published in multiple languages across North America and Europe.

MIX
Paper
FSC® C100212

Printed by Imprimerie Gauvin
Gatineau, Québec